DIVORCE IS WAR
ATTORNEYS ARE CASUALTIES

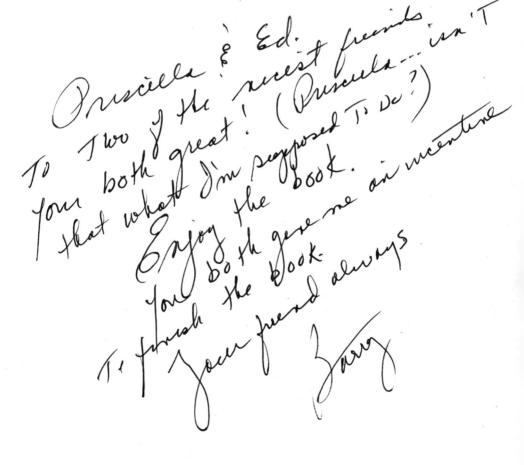

Priscilla & Ed.
To Two of the nicest friends.
Your both great! (Priscilla... isn't
that what I'm supposed to do?)
Enjoy the book.
Your both gave me an incentive
To finish the book.
Your friend always
Barry

DIVORCE IS WAR
ATTORNEYS ARE CASUALTIES

BARRY L. GORDON

Barry L. Gordon

ISBN: 13: 9781530611089
ISBN: 10: 1530611083

Cover design by Timothy Hu, HSU and Associates

Published by Creative Work, Inc.
Chicago, Illinois

Printed in U.S.A.

First U.S. Edition: June 2016

DEDICATION PAGE

To my wife, Jan

ACKNOWLEDGEMENTS

The people who helped me with this book are the people who matter the most to me. First, I want to thank my wife, Jan, for her 49 years of devoted support and the many hours of help she gave me in writing this book.

My daughter and two-time author, Sandy, provided me with a great incentive to write this book. Throughout our lives, I have been competing with her and I think that's been beneficial to both of us. Of course, just once in my life, I'd like to come out on top.

To my son, Paul, I appreciate your everlasting loyalty and your understanding of why I start projects like this. It's true that the fruit never falls far from the tree.

A special thank you to my good friend, Paul Gallender, for the benefit of his insight and advice. He made the process of authoring a book manageable for me.

And to my colleagues in the divorce arena of the legal profession, thank you for your help and guidance, and for helping me become a better attorney.

PROLOGUE

Little did I know I was going to be the lead story on the 6:00 News. My life and career were about to be ruined. My family and friends would be disgraced along with me. I already knew what looking down the barrel of a loaded gun felt like from my days in the Army, but this felt even worse. I had one chance to protect myself and time was of the essence.

I approached the 30th floor offices of the New York State Appellate Division at 27 Madison Avenue. I was facing a 5:00 p.m. deadline to file a "Motion to Impound" all the pleadings or documents in my case. I didn't want the public to know that I had been implicated in this, especially since I thought proving my innocence would be relatively easy to do.

The bombshell that had my name on it was so unexpected that I was a little late in getting my documents ready to file. The Clerk for the Appellate Division had apparently been waiting for me for the better part of an hour. He took the documents to an area behind closed doors. For 15 minutes I stood at the counter, projecting an air of patience which I hoped would mask the unadulterated sense of fear I was experiencing. The Clerk came out and told me that my Motion had been denied because it arrived a few minutes late.

Now I knew my picture was going to be on the 6:00 News. I left the Appellate Division's offices in a daze. It was a typically hot summer day and the perspiration poured off my face. My head was pounding and my heart was racing. On the elevator ride to the lobby, I sought guidance from my inner self as to my next move. Do I call my wife? My kids? Better they hear what was about to happen from me than to be blindsided by watching the news.

As I exited the building I could feel the rapid onset of depression. I know I could never kill myself but at that moment, I couldn't help thinking that it might be an option at some point. Why do people feel so bad when they know they're innocent? Probably because they know they're innocent! The public will pre-judge me and they'll do it knowing exactly nothing about my case. Ain't life grand!

I felt like I was being subjected to military justice in which defendants are presumed guilty until proven otherwise. Is it fair that an attorney's integrity, honesty and character can be impugned and shredded by a single accusation, no matter how outrageous or unsupportable that accusation might be? Of course it's not fair but no segment of the legal profession falls victim to this periodic miscarriage of justice more than divorce attorneys.

My name is Phil Walters and I know of what I speak. You see, I'm a casualty.

Chapter 1

LAWYERS ARE THE REAL VICTIMS

Divorce law is a hot bed of emotion. People who hire an attorney are often extremely emotional and vindictive. Some want to nail their spouses no matter how much it costs; they want to teach them a lesson and they want them to learn it the hard way. Children become collateral damage when revenge is the order of the day. At hearings, some women will buy new clothes and have their hair done so they'll look terrific and make their husbands jealous. It's as if they're saying, "Hey, I've improved myself since I left you," and do they ever flaunt it!

Because of Facebook and other social media, clients take out their vindictiveness on their spouses by posting pictures of them that are awkward at best, and salacious at worst. Women will post pictures of their husbands dressed in women's clothing, or in bed with another man. Men will post graphic sexual photos of their wives which they took in preparation for just such an occasion. It's amazing the lengths that people will go to avoid taking responsibility for their role in a failed marriage. Logic, reason and sanity somehow manage to remain undisturbed and underutilized. The temporary gratification they experience through vengeance means more to them than the fact that what they posted online will haunt their spouses for the rest of their lives. For some people, it's apparently not enough to ruin someone's life for five, ten or fifteen years. They'd rather ruin it all.

There are two types of custody in New York. Joint sharing of decisions is not the same as physical sharing of children. We call kids from these marriages "bag children," because they have to go to school with a bag of clothes so they can go to the other parent's house. There are times when they don't know if it's mommy's day or daddy's day. They're passed around like footballs and they feel that nobody loves them. They have two sets of rules, clothes, dressers and instructions. This kind of thing doesn't go on in every divorce, but it's a commonplace occurrence among my clientele.

One of my clients got her husband to sign what we call a "settlement agreement," and I sent him notice that he would have to appear in court. Generally, the spouses never show up to court once they've signed the agreement. I was in front of the judge with my client when her husband ran in screaming that it was all a fraud and he never signed the agreement. I whispered to my client, "Let's go to a more private room," and we found an empty conference room in the building. I told her she should kiss her husband's ass, be nice to him, and he'd sign the agreement again. Well, they sat down and after he had composed himself, she said to him, "Fuck you, you fucking bastard," and went into a rant throwing every name in the book at him. Can't say I didn't try!

People can actually avoid the acrimony and histrionics that accompany a divorce. There is a divorce publication in the state of New York where you can publish the name of your spouse for four or five weeks and be granted a divorce. There's no division of their assets in these cases. It's easier and cheaper than the alternative but a large percentage of people forego this option for fear of being swindled by a conniving and deceitful spouse.

If you ask 150 lawyers if they find the practice of law fulfilling, I guarantee you that 90 percent will give you an emphatic "No". They'll tell you the practice of law is exhausting and not a source of enjoyment. You make a living but you get stiffed a great deal of the time. It's almost impossible to practice law without walking on eggshells around clients who are wound much too tightly. People don't say thank you and they certainly do not show you love. They may like you, but as soon as difficulties arise, they begin to take it out on you. As a lawyer, if you can count the number of clients who hate you at any given time on just one of your hands, you consider yourself grateful.

Nobody wants to go into divorce law today. They'd have to be out of their minds to do it. Most attorneys will tell you they have problems every minute of every hour. Attorneys become very narrow minded and we only see what we do during the day. The rest of the world becomes non-existent. If you're a trial lawyer and you have to go to court on Monday, you have to be in your office all day Sunday preparing. On Sunday night, you'll see a lot of lights on in the offices of attorneys. There is no break; you're there during lunch preparing witnesses and you need to be there in the evening preparing witnesses. There are no rewards unless you actually win the trial in a personal injury case and get a percentage of it. The practice of law has doubled or tripled in the last 50 years, because of all the paperwork that is required. Law clerks go to court to file documents for you and that is a big expense. My last office had over a million dollars in overhead, and I only had five attorneys working for me.

You get new stuff thrown at you each time you talk to a divorce client. The issues are many and they have to be worked out and placed into a settlement agreement. You need to obtain information, then you need to research the information that's been given to you. After your initial consultation with your client, you're going to do a lot of work sorting through the paperwork, because lots of issues need to be addressed, resolved, and laid out in specific detail in a settlement agreement. Anything that's purchased after the marriage is called Marital Property. Things purchased by a spouse before the marriage are off the table in the negotiations.

There are many aspects of handling a divorce which involve making changes that help your clients, their families, their children, and their relationship to others. Whether the issues are problems about child custody, visitation or division of property, lower income and middle income divorce clients are basically the same. Most live day to day and do not accumulate any savings. It's very difficult for them to hire a professional, like a doctor or a lawyer, and to be able to pay them on a regular basis.

Divorce lawyers have a very difficult time getting paid. People don't have legal insurance like they have medical insurance. So lawyers have to put in 60 to 120 hours of work on some cases, knowing full well collecting their fees is going to be a major problem. People aren't going to drop $20,000 on you. You're lucky if you get $1,000 down, of which $543 has to go to court costs. So, you work out an installment arrangement and they fall behind very quickly. Before you know it, they owe you five grand and if you're lucky if you get fifty cents on the dollar. Wealthier clients don't pay as well as you would think, and they're always behind in their payments, too.

This leads to disharmony between lawyers and clients and creates a conflict of interest between the two parties. Many clients turn to the Departmental Disciplinary Commission (DDC). The DDC is appointed by the Appellate Division of the Supreme Court. It's a voluntary committee that investigates and prosecutes any complaints that warrant disciplinary action. Clients who are upset with their situation often report their attorneys for some crazy reason that they made up. They despise us almost as much as they despise their spouses. Most divorce lawyers have to be on their toes all the time when a client enters their reception area, because they might be carrying a gun. We demand that every client leave his or her gun or knife in a box we provide them with before going to court. We do that because in the 1970s, an attorney walked into the courtroom with his wheelchair-bound client. The case was called and the client wheeled up to the bench, took out a gun and shot the lawyer and the Judge dead. From that day on, everybody is now searched. There is a plaque on the wall for this judge, but they didn't have enough respect for the lawyer to give him a plaque, too. Collateral damage, I guess.

To my amazement, there are these little one bullet pistols that women carry in their purses in the lower income neighborhoods. I know this because many clients forget to pick them up at our office after the court session. There's always a huge amount of unclaimed knives, as well. Of course, some women use weapons that can't be checked at the door. On that note, my story begins.

Chapter 2

THE DAY MY LIFE CHANGED

I had been practicing law in New York for 13 years before meeting Afshan, a woman who would impact my career and my life in ways that I never imagined. Things started out smoothly enough, but I had trouble making sense of her heavy Middle Eastern accent. Originally, I didn't know where she was from and I had little experience with her region's culture.

I never assume that immigrants think and live like Americans because the differences are often quite dramatic. I experienced the culture of India through one of my clients. When individuals from India get divorced, they bring their uncle and grandma to the initial consultation and will make no decisions unless everyone in the family agrees. They'll come back several times more when another uncle pops up and wants to take part in the discussions. I respect their culture and traditions.

No matter how people choose to end a marriage, their reasons for doing so have more in common than not. I would help them like I helped everyone else. That's the mindset I had when I accepted Afshan as a client. Actually, that mindset is the main reason I got into divorce law in the first place.

It was June 1, 1988 when Afshan came to my firm seeking a divorce. Her physical appearance was distracting at first. She was dressed in a flimsy tank top with a low-cut V-neck which revealed a far too generous amount of cleavage of her huge chest. She was about 5'4" and weighed maybe 120 pounds. It seemed as though she never took her eyes off of me at that first consultation. I know now that she was trying to get an accurate reading of me as quickly as possible.

We require our clients to fill out a questionnaire in their own handwriting. We do this because if they end up denying anything, we have something with which to defend ourselves. She completed the paperwork in 15 minutes. Afshan was first seen by my associate, Carolyn Rogers, an attorney with five years of experience. The questionnaire showed that Afshan was 30 years old and had been unemployed for seven years. She listed her spouse as 33 and the owner of a 7-11 franchise. Their tax returns showed earnings of approximately $25,000 per year. They had two children, ages five and one, and had been married five years. They had been separated for one year.

Afshan knew almost nothing about her husband's business dealings. She had no idea what bank accounts her husband had and her own personal account contained less than $500. Rambling fast in her broken English, she told me, "He leave. He heet me. Here, here," she said pointing to her neck area. With that low-cut top I had to be quick to not stare at her breasts which were practically popping out of her shirt. It was distracting. She told me that her husband left her after that particular instance of abuse. He pushed her against the wall, struck her on the arm and attempted to choke her. I told her to see her doctor and the visit became part of her legal record.

Afshan and her husband, Belin, were born in Iran and came to America in 1978. Their cultural background played an important part in their psychological makeups. He came from the lower merchant class. After centuries of bad dealings, he and his class became suspicious of everyone. Lying, deception and manipulation weren't considered evil; rather, they became necessary skills for a merchant to master. Belin had mastered those skills long before he came to America, and he soon learned that those skills were far more lucrative here than they were in Iran. His was a cash business and Belin knew just how profitable such a venture could be, if you knew how to game the system. Belin found that gaming the system in America was far easier and much less dangerous here than in his repressive native land.

Afshan faced the same fate as most Middle Eastern women, which is second-class status and being completely dependent upon and ruled by her husband. Afshan was deeply affected by her new country and its different view of a woman's place. Women had power in their new homeland and that's one of the things about America that Belin despised. Women were little more than indentured servants to him in Iran and he saw no reason to change his opinion of them after coming to America. It was simply the way of the world, as he saw it.

Afshan prided herself on knowing her rights as an American. She wanted a divorce, but she was unemployed and needed financial support for herself and her children. My office filed for what we call a Petition for Dissolution of Marriage (a divorce) on June 27, 1990. It stated they both spouses were residents of the State of New York for more than 90 days. It gave the date of their marriage and their children's date of birth. It affirmed that neither child was adopted and that she was not pregnant. The grounds for divorce cited repeated episodes of mental cruelty. We could have added physical cruelty, too, but that is harder to prove. We didn't push infidelity, because that's even more difficult to prove. The petition requested that Afshan be assigned her non-marital property and asked the court to justly divide their marital property. She sought both temporary and permanent custody of their minor children along with child support and maintenance. There was nothing at all unusual about any of this. At this point, she was just another client who could no longer bear living in a loveless, abusive marriage. To say that I've had many, many clients like Afshan would be an understatement.

A week after we filed her petition, I received a letter from Afshan indicating that she and her husband were back together and attempting to reconcile. She requested that we drop the divorce and that I stop representing her. She thanked my firm for taking her case and assured us she would call in the future if there were other problems. I was ready for this. In the throes of divorce, women often cling to any hope of reconciliation. On the other hand, maybe it was for real. In any case, at the time she wrote her letter she owed us a very small balance of attorney's fees, an amount too small to worry about collecting.

Their reconciliation reunion turned out to be a fragile one. Four weeks later she called our office and said her husband had kicked her out after another fight and she wanted to proceed with the divorce. I got what I needed from her to prepare an Affidavit in support for a Petition for an Order of Protection. In theory, once an Order of Protection is granted, it can restrain a spouse from having any contact with the Petitioner. The Judge has the authority to place temporary custody of the children with one of the parties and to exclude the other spouse from any contact with the children, as well as ordering him to vacate their home.

The Order was granted ex-parte, meaning without having both spouses present. Her husband wasn't notified because there was the possibility that he might harm her. This, too, happens a lot, so it's standard procedure to protect one of them and it's almost always the wife. The thought of Afshan being physically harmed bothered me, but that was a common reaction of mine when it came to abused female clients.

The petition for Order of Protection alleged that Belin had moved out of their home. It stated he had sole authority to deposit and withdraw money from various bank accounts, all of which were unknown to her. She insisted he had taken the money out of their various accounts and hid them in safe deposit boxes in an attempt to avoid paying taxes and to cheat her out of her fair share. It further alleged that even before they had separated, he said to her, "You will never know how much money I have. You will never find where I put the money. I have taken the money out of the American Mainstream Bank. You will pay for your mistake. You're nothing without me, I'll make sure you're never anything more than a whore." He taunted her that she would never be able to stop him, because she wouldn't have sufficient money to retain an attorney. He was the one with the assets and he planned to exploit that as much as possible. He had taken both of their cars and refused to allow her to use one. She had to grocery shop and look for a job by walking or taking the bus with her two children. He sounded like a "Class A jerk."

One day, Afshan stated that her husband brutally beat her on several occasions. He had kicked and punched her numerous times. She showed me the bruises, yelling, "What kind of man do this! Not American man. He poosh me. He poosh me," she said, demonstrating the abuse by dramatically falling to the floor, a moved which exposed way too much of her thighs. I helped her up and she clung to me. I comforted her for a few seconds, thinking it would have been cruel not to. She told me than an ambulance took her to the hospital after one of his attacks. Her husband followed her to the hospital and brought her home after treatment. After arriving back at the house, the argument heated up again and he threw her outside, without a jacket, on a cold, rainy evening. He locked her out for more than three hours. She alleged that he owned two guns and frequently threatened her with them. The police were called on several occasions and she gave specific dates when the abuse took place.

Orders of Protection are granted routinely by judges. They aren't as concerned about the specifics of the Order or the allegations being made against a person, as they are in protecting their own butt by granting them. They don't want to see their picture in the newspaper if, after they denied an Order of Protection, one of the parties committed a battery on the other. The Sheriff's Department served the husband on July 12, 1987. Shortly thereafter, we had a hearing with the husband and his attorney, Rod Schalkin, at which I scheduled a conference with all parties in my office.

Schalkin arrived for the settlement conference and we shook hands. He was a heavyset man, around 5'8" and weighed about 215. He showed me that he was not a man to be pushed around. There was a slight nervousness about him and he frequently wiped sweat from his balding head. Still, he spoke with authority. Since he didn't send a young associate to my office, I figured that he was a sole practitioner and the weight of this case was on him alone.

He said his client earned $1,500 to $2,000 per week, and apparently didn't report most of it to the IRS. Schalkin only disclosed this fact because the wife had filed a joint tax return with his client. If his income became an issue, she, too, would be in jeopardy for signing a fraudulent tax return. We talked briefly about the possibility of reconciliation. Rod said the husband thought his wife was very flirtatious and would disappear in the evenings, leaving him with both children. He was highly suspicious of his wife and became extremely jealous. Shouting matches were common. In spite of the money he was making and the new freedoms he enjoyed, there were times when Belin

longed for the power and control over women that he used to
have back home.

Afshan and Belin were in the conference room waiting
for the Settlement Conference to proceed. Belin was slim
and had a dark complexion. Like many Iranian men he had an
untrimmed black moustache extending into his cheeks, dark
black eyes and thick eyebrows. He was polite and appeared to
have respect for me and his attorney. As Rod and I were talking, we heard fierce screaming and yelling coming from the
adjacent office where we found our clients almost at each other's throats. They were bickering in their native language. We
separated them for a few minutes to let things cool off. Then
all four of us returned to the conference room. When Rod and
I left the room for a moment to discuss something, we heard a
loud commotion and again had to separate the two parties. At
that moment, I thought about the misfortune of their children
having to learn life's lessons from two such unstable and hate-
ful parents. If those kids have a chance of succeeding in life,
it's a slim one at best.

I indicated what issues I thought were on the table and what
needed to be discussed. Custody of the children was first and
foremost. Because he worked such long and uncertain hours,
Belin said he would concede custody to his wife if it came down
to an actual fight. He wanted his wife to waive maintenance, or
what is known as alimony. His wife needed to get back on her
feet, and would have to acquire some new skills to find a job and
support herself. I said it would take her at least a year to do that,
but I had a feeling my estimate was probably low.

We agreed he would support her with maintenance in the amount of $600 per month. However, it was to last for only six months. He agreed to pay child support in the amount of 28% of his net income. We agreed on $85 per week for their two children. The issues of visitation were more or less boilerplate. He would have visitation every other weekend from 5 p.m. on Friday to 6 p.m. on Sunday, and on alternate holidays. The husband would pay a maximum of $1,500 of his wife's attorney's fees. He agreed to be responsible for all of the couple's outstanding debts, and would pay his wife's rent for a year.

I wasn't happy with the figures that the husband said he was earning, but the only way we could verify the actual amounts would be to spend a great deal of time and money by hiring a CPA. That would take at least four more months and would cost thousands of dollars in attorney's and accountant's fees. I was concerned that Afshan might come back later and claim she didn't get enough money or that we didn't do sufficient discovery to determine his true income. So, I had her sign what we call a "protect your ass" agreement. It basically stated she was willing to proceed with the settlement agreement in spite of my recommendation that we turn him upside down and inside out to find out his true income. The agreement she signed said she had refused to follow my recommendations. I was confident that the letter would protect me. She waited in my office for fifteen minutes until her husband and her attorney were safely gone before leaving.

It's always sad to see two people who once loved each other and had so much hope for the future, end up in divorce court. However, my sympathy was misplaced. Little did I know that this wasn't the end of the case, nor would it be the end of my relationship with this woman. I was about to find out just how far some people can reach into another person's life and how much havoc they can wreak as long as they're willing to lie.

The final court hearing is where the Petitioner has to testify about the contents of the Agreement. This enables the Judge to make a decision as to whether or not the Agreement is fair. If the Judge deems it so, he or she will enter a Judgment for Dissolution of Marriage and sever the bonds of matrimony, thereby making the divorce official.

The courtroom is a chaotic place. There may be as many as 75 people present at all times. A judge hears up to 50 cases each morning so there isn't much time to give anybody. Most people don't know that lawyers set up their own schedule and court dates, rather than the judge. Of course, we coordinate closely with the Judge's scheduler. Everyone is nervous and we try to prepare the clients for their testimony before we go to the courtroom. There is a bailiff in the courtroom at all times, He's a kind of keeper of the peace because there have been cases of violence where crazed litigants have gone on killing sprees. Nowadays, everyone has to go through a scanner to check for weapons when they enter the courthouse. Other kinds of violence against lawyers and court personnel sometimes take place elsewhere. Auto vandalism is not uncommon. I once had my car covered with Hershey chocolates. Other lawyers have had their tires slashed or salt poured in their gas tanks.

Afshan came into the courtroom on the day of her final hearing wearing a fairly risque outfit. She wore a very tight sweater, a short skirt, and 2-½ inch heels. Her hair was recently coiffed and she wore a lot of makeup. Most people would guess that she hadn't shed a tear the night before. No, the picture one got of her was that of a prostitute waiting on a corner in the red light district. She wiggled up the twenty feet to the judge's bench with a Marilyn Monroe-like swaying of the hips, and I motioned for her to stand next to me before she was sworn in by the court clerk. Unlike movie depictions, most of the time clients testify standing next to their attorney, rather than taking the stand.

I took over from there and used my opening statement to give the Judge a glimpse of what to expect. Brevity is the key in any court proceeding because of the large volume of cases. I proceeded to ask the boilerplate type of questions that the judge wanted to hear. He heard the same questions fifty to sixty times a day, fifty two weeks a year. This judge was familiar with me because I had appeared before him hundreds of times. I didn't go into any extreme detail with my statement. I had prepped my client prior to this hearing to say yes or no to all of my questions. I phrased 90% of them so she would say yes.

The questions were framed so as to not inflame the husband or his attorney. I never look to create disharmony. I'm simply trying to get people the divorce they want, and to travel that road as smoothly as possible. I'm looking to walk out of that courtroom with a Judgment for Divorce, nothing more and nothing less. The grounds of mental cruelty are the easiest to prove because you can use anything that indicates that the client or Petitioner's life has been adversely affected by the actions of the spouse. Under mental cruelty, my client only needed to show was that she felt despondent and suffered from headaches or sleep deprivation as a result of the husband's verbal abuse.

Suddenly, Belin stood up and yelled, "I don't want a divorce! I love her!" Such an outburst is actually rather common in divorce cases. Sometimes it's hard not to break out in laughter when you know how badly the guy treated his wife. It was a mistake by his lawyer not to have prepared his client to keep his emotions under control. The judge looked the husband in the eye and said, "Sir, if you don't agree, I will stop the proceedings, and maybe you and your wife can go to counseling." Schalkin immediately asked the judge for two minutes with his client. He advised the husband not to say anything else and the man reluctantly agreed.

Afshan relied on our pre-court preparation in answering all of my questions. Then it was time for the husband's attorney to question her. He basically asked his questions so that his name was on the record that he was present and did his duty in representing his client. The divorce could have taken place without him, but it's important for an attorney to show his client the transcript indicating he was there and had represented him. His questions got Afshan to say that these decisions were solely hers and nobody else's. He got her to affirm that she participated in the negotiations of the Agreement, so that she couldn't complain later that it was the lawyers' makings, and not hers. "Your honor," said Schalkin, "I am satisfied and I will turn this matter over to counsel for the wife." I then handed the judge the

Judgment for Dissolution of Marriage and asked him to sign the Judgment and agree to it.

The Judge touched on a couple of other minor matters of the Agreement and stated, "I hereby Order by this court that the bonds of matrimony are forever dissolved. Transcripts to be filed with this Court within 28 days. Counsel, please fill out the appropriate orders." I gave three copies of the Judgment to the clerk whose job was to place the Circuit Court Clerk's stamp on the last page. The signed document was recorded in the "minute book" kept on the judge's desk and downloaded into his computer. Now it was my job to sit down and fill out a "Court Order," per the terms the Judge had ordered.

Unbeknownst to most people, Judges do not write out or type Court Orders. It's always the lawyers who do it per the Judge's instructions and hand it to him for their signature. The same thing applies to Jury Instructions. Juries think the Judge has written the instructions, though it's the lawyers who type out the Jury Instructions and the opposing counsel bicker as to which one should be submitted. There are no juries in divorce cases. The judge makes a decision in his chambers as to the submission of those instructions.

There is a wall shelf in the courtroom with 100 slots for various court forms and orders. I checked the box on my form that said the bonds of matrimony had been dissolved and I had 28 days to file the court reporter's transcript of proceeding **in** the judge's chambers. If my transcript is unclear, the court reporter will call me. I'll review it, sign it, and present it to the judge in his chambers. Some judges don't routinely review the transcript once it is presented to them. This is especially true in lower income or middle class divorces where the assets are of little value.

As we left the courtroom, I handed my client a stamped copy of the "Judgment for Dissolution of Marriage." I told her she was now divorced, but her husband had 30 days to file a Petition to Vacate the Marriage. But it's an entirely new ballgame if new evidence is acquired after 30 days. My client gladly took the copy I gave her. Some litigants become extremely depressed at this time while others are joyful. There used to be a family member with the litigant on the day of the divorce. Usually, this is kept as a private matter. I have to assume there is some shame to the process even today.

We parted in the courtroom and went our separate ways. I had other cases waiting for my attention. Little did I know that this parting was actually the end of the beginning and the beginning of the end.

Chapter 3

LAW AS A LIFE JACKET

I grew up in a dysfunctional family. I'd call it an early pre-law course for a future divorce attorney, and what I learned stayed with me for the rest of my life.

Divorce attorneys spend three years in school learning the law and spend the rest of their careers getting an education. I'm pretty sure that many family attorneys will tell you the practice of divorce law takes over your life. My childhood gave me a little shortcut, but, in retrospect, it was more of a curse than a blessing.

I've saved a lot of marriages of friends who wanted divorces. I'd go over to their houses and calm them down and make sure they didn't get divorced. I was their friend. They trusted me because I knew them long before things began to go south between them. I'd spend time counseling them, trying to convince them not to pay me to change their lives because I knew that they could work it out. I always want to save the marriage.

I guess I'm not a typical businessman because of that. But I know a good marriage is worth hanging onto.

Fifteen years ago, I received a letter from a woman who came to me seeking a divorce many years before. Susan Thomas wanted it very badly but I refused to take her case. She was a beautiful woman, in her thirties, career-driven and determined. I spent time with her in my office where she told me about her life and described her sadness. She was ready to write me a check, but I said no. I advised her to go on a vacation with her husband and then come back to see me.

Twelve years later I received a six-page handwritten letter in the mail from Susan Thomas. She went on and on about how patient I was with her. She had been so angry with me for not taking her case, and for telling me to try to sort it out. But she did go on that vacation. And in this lovely letter she told me that I was responsible for the three beautiful children that she had and she thanked me for making it possible. She acknowledged how different her life would have been today had I not insisted she give their marriage another chance. Successes like Susan's were the highlights in a legal career where highlights were few and far between.

I've been practicing law for 48 years and I've seen it all. I had one case where a woman called me and said her husband had a rifle to her head and he told her he was going to pull the trigger in ten seconds. He did, and then he shot himself.

One woman said her husband forced her to have sex with any of his friends who walked through the door, and he would watch. One husband locked my client in a closet for three days, feeding her only bread and water. Then, for some reason which I could not grasp, he stuck a broomstick up his wife's vagina. A large amount of husbands beat the shit out of their wives and some wives either beat the shit out of their husbands or stab them.

I had an airline pilot call me at four in the morning but he wouldn't tell me all the details. He said he would pay me handsomely, because he needed a divorce and he needed it quickly. He came in with an overcoat on and it wasn't winter. His wife had stabbed him 16 times during the night and he had just left the emergency room when he called me. He had a flight later than morning on a 747 from New York to a foreign country. He said he'd put the overcoat on and no one would be any the wiser.

One client of mine had multiple personalities. I'll call her Jane. She was a very pretty woman who came to me for a divorce. I asked her to get a letter from her psychiatrist to show that she was legally competent to testify, and she did that. She was very sweet and normal until she asked to use one of our telephones before we left for court. I obliged and left her alone. When I told her we had to leave in ten minutes, she grimaced in a way that I'd never seen before. "I'll get off when I get off," she said rudely, so I walked away. A few minutes later she was back with a smiley face and was very sweet. After the court hearing, I asked her if she would provide me with information on multiple personalities so I could read about it.

Jane had five different personalities, each of whom had a different name. All of them were there to protect her. She became Mary when she was on the phone. The question I had later, after she had been divorced, was did we divorce Mary or Jane? It's a very good legal question for the husband. Probably a good bar exam question, too.

We've had many clients who have been married two or three times but didn't bother to get divorced from anyone. That made them all bigamists. They didn't care because nobody else in society cared, even though a state's attorney could have filed charges against them. The question is who would file the complaint so it's something that's usually just left alone. But there have been times when people would come in, mostly men, and admit they were bigamists who would like to get divorced from the first wife, even though they're married to the second wife. It became an urgent matter because the second wife found out about the first wife and went to the courthouse and looked it up and found there had been no divorce between the first wife and the husband. So, the second wife thinks her marriage is void, which it is, by law. In order to make things clear we go in and vacate the marriage to the first wife and proceed with that divorce. Then, we let him remarry the second wife. Lots of issues arise from that situation but since they're all the product of a faulty first premise, I'll spare you the ridiculous details.

I've had hundreds of clients whose spouses would vandalize a car in ways that would never occur to you. One of my clients owned 67 pieces of slum property and refused to tell his wife where they were or how much equity he owned in them. There was a guy who was sexually abusing his girlfriend's four-year-old daughter. Then, for some inexplicable reason, he started making threats on the President of the United States and...wait for it...ME! I ended up working with the Secret Service and they eventually caught the guy. While they were looking for the guy, they were in my office quite often.

A woman came into our office and told us her husband worked in a factory where they cut up chickens. The chickens get placed on a conveyor belt and the husband accidentally got caught on the belt and died after suffering severe wounds. We thought it was a great Worker's Comp case until we learned that she had already gone to six other lawyers and filed the same case. The ironic part was that the whole story was made up. Her husband was never on a conveyer belt, he was never cut up, and he was never killed. Clients tend to try to put everything past you in personal injury and divorce cases.

Occasionally, the practice of divorce law provides some much needed humor to the proceedings. A seventy-year-old woman came to my office for a divorce. We went to court but her husband failed to appear. I was trying to establish the grounds of what her husband did wrong, when she said the following: "He stuck his wing ding in me, in my mouth." Then she put both hands up to the sides of her face and pushed her head from the left to the right. "He went swoosh, swoosh, swoosh, with his wing ding," she said. I'm not sure she understood why the entire courtroom erupted into hysterical laughter. Truth be told, clients like her are a refreshing change from the kind of manipulative behavior I faced on a daily basis.

Chapter 4

THE ACCUSATIONS AGAINST ME!

The transcript was ready fifteen days after the hearing and I sent my clerk over to pick it up. I was looking for something that would pop out to a judge as inappropriate or incorrect, but I found nothing. A month later I received a letter from Belin's attorney, Rod Schalkin. His client had advised him that his wife wouldn't let him pick up the children at 1 p.m. on Saturday. She switched it to Friday at 5 p.m. The Friday time conflicted with his work schedule and Schalkin asked me to try and work it out with her.

At first Afshan wasn't agreeable to changing the schedule. "Every child needs and has a right to a father," I told her. Situations like this are always a real challenge because of a client's emotions, vindictiveness and coldness towards their ex. But, I got her to agree to cooperate and that temporarily calmed the post-divorce waters.

Thirty days later she contacted my office and said her husband was one-month behind in his child support payments. Since he no longer had an attorney, I sent a letter directly to him. I told him one of the children had to stop attending private school because the tuition payments weren't being made. I said he was in violation of the Judgment for Dissolution of Marriage and gave him 10 days to remedy the situation, before I asked that he be held in contempt of court.

Three days later I heard from Belin's new attorney, Tom Patterson. He claimed that his client was not being granted his visitation rights per the Agreement. He alleged that Belin had attempted to visit the children for the past several months but Afshan had refused him contact. She was angry that he was now living with another woman. The petition asked that my client be held in contempt of Court for violating the visitation agreement. I wrote to her immediately and said his request to see his children didn't seem unreasonable. I reminded her that her ex-husband was allowed to see other women sexually as long as there was no sexual activity while the children were present, but that it was okay for him to have another woman on the premises.

Many women who get sole custody apparently feel that the children came into this world without any help from the father and therefore do not need his presence after a divorce. Female litigants also think that waiving child support takes away the husband's visitation rights, but it doesn't. Such thinking completely fails to take into account the importance and significance of the relationship between a father and his children. I told her I agreed with Belin's proposed visitation schedule.

One day I received a voice message from Afshan. She wasn't raving but she was very determined. "I will not allow him to have any visitation," she said with conviction. "To hell with him. I want no more child support. He can keep his money!" I phoned her back and she wasn't happy about the tone of my voice or the content of my message. "The judge will order your husband to pay child support for the children. You cannot prevent that. The visitation is for the children, not for you," I said firmly. I wanted it on the record that this was her opinion and that she refused to follow my recommendations. I told her I wanted to see her in my office at 8:15 on the morning of her court hearing date. I was confident I could get her to listen to reason.

Two days before her court date, I received correspondence from the Departmental Disciplinary Commission (DDC). Every lawyer cringes at the thought of receiving an envelope in the mail from the DDC because as an investigatory body created by the Supreme Court to investigate attorneys who violate the rules, a letter from them is never going to be a happy one. Even though its commonplace and divorce lawyers receive the most Complaints filed with the DDC, they still cringe upon receipt of such an envelope. I cringed. Most attorneys compare the DDC to a Gestapo organization because both groups more or less wield absolute power.

I couldn't think of anybody who would have any reason to file a Complaint with the DDC. When I saw Afshan's name on the Complaint, the worst-case scenario came to mind. The Complaint was a "Request for Investigation of a Lawyer". It was in her handwriting and she said the following things about me:

"He refuses to return my calls. He hangs up the phone when I can reach him. He is arrogant and sassy to me with smart-alecky comments. A complaint from my ex-husband was not answered and I was not fully advised about the support agreement before divorce action. He is impatient with me and inconsiderate of my problems. He always gave me late-afternoon appointments, even though I requested mornings. He put his hands on me four times. He grabbed me and hugged me and propositioned me to go to a hotel with him. I pushed him away and told him he was married. There were many vulgar actions and he locked the door and exposed himself to me three or four times." Under her signature, it said, "This is not complete - more will follow in a separate letter." More will follow?!

I was devastated. It was that last point that really scared me. I couldn't concentrate and walked around in a daze for the rest of the day, unresponsive to my staff. All sorts of questions began flooding my mind. What is my wife and my family going to think? Will my wife leave me? How can I explain this situation to my children? I needed to get a hold of myself and to think rationally. My life and career were at stake. For some reason, Afshan had turned on me with a vengeance. Before long, I would learn this list of her complaints was merely the tip of the iceberg!

There's an old lawyer's cliche that says, "If you have yourself for a client, you have a fool for a client." Truer words have never been spoken. Still, finding the right attorney was and is no easy task. There was no book you could go to and find out who was the best in a particular field of law. There was no Yelp app to search online for attorney reviews. You went by your colleagues' opinions, which were mostly hearsay. If any of my colleagues and friends had severe problems with the DDC, I wouldn't know about it unless it became public and was published in the local attorney periodicals. It's not something a lawyer in trouble publicizes to his peers. The last thing I wanted to do was to ask my colleagues if they had any first-hand information about addressing a complaint with the DDC. If I did, they would have immediately known I was in trouble.

I've always made quick and decisive decisions but that trait has landed me in hot water on numerous occasions. I realized this was too important for me to risk having an inexperienced attorney handle it. I knew I needed one who specialized in representation at the DDC and I needed that person as soon as possible. I wanted to get this colossal weight off my shoulders. I had become completely dysfunctional. It felt like I was being thrust into the role of a villain in a play whose script had not yet been written. But I knew that my character would not be a popular one and that meant I needed to act fast.

I scheduled an appointment with the very prominent criminal defense firm of Benson, Steinhouser and Sterling. The 36 hours before my appointment would be the worst 36 hours of my life. Unfortunately, I'd be expressing that sentiment a lot over the next several months. The apprehension of waiting for each hour to pass was more disabling than the previous one. I started to become very short tempered with my staff and anything would set me off. Communicating with my wife and children at home was almost impossible. I just wanted to be alone.

As far as I was concerned, my life was over and the feeling kept getting worse.

It was a lonely two-mile walk to my new attorney's office. I felt like I was marching down death row to my execution. The sense of doom I was experiencing was palpable, even at this early stage of the proceedings. Thank God there was no one in the reception area when I got there. When you find yourself in the offices of high-powered defense attorneys, the reason you're there is almost always bad and everyone knows it. I didn't want anyone to see me there, anyone at all. Even the 15-minute wait on the leather chair was excruciatingly long.

Steinhouser appeared to have broken his nose at some point in his life and I thought he might have boxed in his younger years. He was very outgoing and his personality made me feel at home. "I don't really know where to start," I said. "Ever hear of a mouthpiece with nothing to say?" It was a lame attempt at humor. I took out my file and said, "This is all bullshit! I didn't do any of these sexual things. I told her she must let her ex-husband see the children and she had a real problem with that. She didn't like what I told her and the next day she filed the Complaint with the DDC alleging all this bullshit." The outburst was cathartic for me, at least for the moment. I was finally able to open a valve and let the fear and frustration come out.

Steinhouser was all business. He started taking notes as we went through my file piece by piece. We talked about the initial conference with my Associates in my firm, the possible reconciliation with Afshan and Belin, her calling off the case, the re-instating of the case and the final filing for the divorce. I told him the most important aspect of this matter was that I had admonished my client that she must give visitation to her husband. It was right after that that she went to the DDC with her ludicrous complaint.

"Did you do any of this sexual stuff?" he asked. "No, no, no!" I said, nearly jumping off my chair. "Okay," he said. "Calm down. I can understand how you feel." He indicated that he had represented many clients who faced DDC Complaints, some of which were very serious. Most of his clients were accused of misappropriating client's funds, rather than sexual misconduct. But I'm the type of lawyer who tries to talk his clients out of divorce. I'd never do any of those things she accused me of doing.

We spent two-and-a-half hours together at this initial conference and I felt lighter after I left his office. I was convinced he was the right person for me and I was as satisfied as I could be at this point. I felt like a quarterback who was about to get sacked by the defense. All I could do in that situation was to get rid of the ball before I got hit. He wanted a $10,000 retainer which I thought was outrageous. However, I knew I had to pay it. As my old boss once said, "You'll never get rich as a lawyer, but you'll make a comfortable living." He was right. I wasn't rich, but I could afford $10,000. If I couldn't, I would have borrowed it. I would have done anything to get me out of this nightmare.

I returned to my office and started to pay attention to my law practice. I was breathing better and deeper. I wasn't as volatile as I was in the past week. It felt like the biopsy results had just come back negative. It even felt like I was standing up straighter. Steinhouser will answer the complaint, I thought to myself, and it would satisfy the DDC and put the matter to rest. That feeling wouldn't last long, but the sense of relief certainly felt good.

Four days later, Steinhouser called me back to his office to review the letter he had prepared for the DDC. Based on extensive discussions with me and reviewing all of the documents, he said it was obvious that my client's Complaint was "largely false, extremely malicious, and utterly lacking in foundation. Mr. Walters categorically denies any and all allegations that he ever grabbed, hugged, propositioned or said any disturbing words, or acted in a vulgar way at any time." I had painted a black and white picture for Steinhouser and his letter was written with that in mind.

My case took place at the same time that Supreme Court nominee, Clarence Thomas, was undergoing his confirmation hearings on Capitol Hill in 1991. He had been accused of improper sexual advances by one of his former employees, Anita Hill. Though my situation did not rise to the status of the Thomas-Hill controversy, it seemed to be more than just a coincidence that those hearings were taking place prior to and during the time when my client lodged her complaint with the DDC.

Steinhouser's letter documented my involvement with this client point by point and mentioned everything I had done for her as her divorce attorney. It detailed that I told my client I would write her ex-husband a letter requesting that he clean up his act and be regular with his visitation and payments. My client apparently could not accept that a Court would not prevent a father from visiting with children under these circumstances.

She phoned me again expressing her anger over my inability to prevent visitation. She didn't want to hear what I had to say.

Her list of particulars against me went on and on. "She did not want to hear what Mr. Walters had to say," wrote Steinhouser. He said Afshan would appear in my office without an appointment demanding to see me at once. She resorted to ranting and raving, all of which made little sense. My secretary was unable to calm my client down, nor could any other member of my staff. The other people in the reception area looked like they would have rather been anyplace else. Outbursts like this can destroy a law firm's reputation. I had to explain to her that I was busy with another client and urged her to make an appointment for another day. She scheduled one for a week later but never showed up. I had no further communication with her. Every good effort was made by me and my staff to accommodate her concerns and zealously safeguard her interests.

"Mr. Walters and his office undertook the representation of this client in a professionally proper fashion," concluded Steinhouser. "Every good effort was made to accommodate her concerns, and zealously safeguard her interests. The issues involved in her divorce, like visitation, maintenance and child support, were emotionally charged. Often, such matters are not resolved to the complete satisfaction of the litigant. However, such frustrations do not justify the kind of libelous charges she has labeled against Mr. Walters."

Steinhouser's letter was so good that I actually thought it was going to fly. Once they studied the logic in his letter, surely that would be the end of this episode. I kept my mouth shut. Of course, I was thinking like a client rather than a lawyer. I should have known that the DDC would send my client a copy of the letter before they responded. I shouldn't have been surprised when they started contacting my past female clients to inquire whether or not any "sexual advances" had ever been made by me, but I was.

If the DDC didn't accept Steinhouser's answer, they had the right to take a statement from me in the presence of a court reporter. The statement would be conducted during interrogation or cross-examination and would be akin to a "fishing expedition." Before doing this, they needed to vote a "formal complaint." The complaint filed by the client is only the beginning of an investigation. A formal complaint has to be voted on by a panel selected by the Supreme Court and the DDC, at which point it would become a formal charge against me. I walked to my office feeling quite confident that Steinhouser's letter would be sufficient to dismiss the entire matter. I felt like my house was on solid ground, not realizing that this particular part of it was built on sand.

Afshan was in my office numerous times before the actual divorce hearing. I told her a violation of child visitation is taken very seriously by the Court, but she was resistant to giving him any access to the children. She had no logical reason for being so stubborn because the children were not in harm's way. I suspect it was more or less a way of punishing her ex-husband.

Early on in our meetings she began moving toward my desk until she got next to my chair. There was no reason to inquire why she was doing it; her body language said it all. She came right up to me and made it very clear that she was there to be had. Looking back, there's no question in my mind that this was an attempt at a seduction. I didn't respond, but my hormones were raging. Call it a tease. In fact, call it anything you want, but a seduction by any other name is still a seduction.

She still had a lot of animosity towards her ex-husband and wasn't going to give an inch. Logic would not sway her, nor would her legal responsibility to make sure her husband had visitation of their children. After that last appointment, she constantly called the office as if she had carte blanche authority to talk to me. Completely disregarding protocol, she became so demanding that the receptionist could barely control her. Afshan called three or four times a week, insisting that I drop whatever I was doing and talk to her.

She went so far as to again say she didn't want child support. I reminded her the support was for the children and not for her. She didn't understand the distinction, nor could she conceive of a judge not siding with her. She no longer looked at me with respect. She thought I was her puppet and I would do everything she wanted. I wrote her a letter to put on the record that she must allow her ex-husband visitation rights. The letter laid out the fact that she had refused to follow my advice and that the judge could enter sanctions which could result in her being held in contempt of Court for violating the Judgment of Dissolution of Marriage. I won't deny I was protecting myself because in law, you need to worry about the worst-case scenarios.

During her next visit to my office, she stood up and again came around to my chair. This time she took my hand and pulled it so that I would respond by getting out of the chair. I stood next to her, face to face. She drew me closer. "How could this be going on?" I said to myself. "The door's not locked. Any one of the staff could walk in on this." At that moment, I regained my senses, controlled my emotions, pushed her away and said, "I am a professional and will not tolerate this."

I couldn't tolerate Afshan's abuse and disrespect of my office staff. And I certainly couldn't have her making sexual advances on me. I thought it was time to have a very serious discussion with her about this problem. I was in my office on a Sunday and called her to see if she had time to come down and talk. She did, and there was no one in the office except me. In retrospect, I wish I hadn't called her and I wish I hadn't been alone in the office. What was I thinking? Here I was in the same room with her, with no witnesses and on a Sunday no less.

I told her she couldn't just expect me to drop everything when she called and that unscheduled visits were a problem. She needed to also understand that trying to appeal to my male instincts was not welcome and would not work.

The words seemed to hit her hard. And although that's where it ended, it wasn't what she told the DDC. "He want to go to a hotel with me," she said. "He said, I love you. I miss you. He exposed himself to me three times or four." She lied but I would never have believed that her word would be enough to ruin my life.

I found myself in a major dilemma. I had told my attorney to deny all her allegations because nothing "significant" had taken place, at least by me. It was she who made advances towards me, advances which I quickly and firmly rebuffed. However, I didn't mention any of this to my attorney. I knew he'd have to pull a rabbit out of a hat to get me out of this. I also knew he wouldn't be pleased that I hadn't told him of my client's attempts to seduce me; that I had taken matters into my own hands and called her to my office on a Sunday. I couldn't fool myself any more into thinking this wasn't going to be a major problem. On the bright side, I seemed to be an expert at administering self-inflicted wounds.

I prefaced my remarks to Steinhouser by saying how much trauma that this episode had brought to my life. "I still maintain that there are as many holes in her story as a leaky sieve," I said. He was a lot more understanding that I had expected, yet he showed his disappointment in voice and demeanor. We both concluded that Afshan was extremely seductive by design and intent. However, I was still left with the problem of explaining to the DDC why I didn't show my defense from the beginning. I knew the DDC wouldn't be as compassionate with me as Steinhouser was.

Changing my story created a major problem on top of the problem I had been facing. My credibility had been tarnished and I was treated as if I didn't deserve any respect. Steinhouser interrogated me and was more guarded in his questioning. I wondered if he thought I was guilty. Together we considered one scenario after another as to how the DDC would react to me after learning I hadn't disclosed her sexual advances. We didn't make any final decisions but I gave him total discretion to send the appropriate letter and fight for me. I came back to my office feeling like a little boy lost in the big world. I was no longer a "big man," the Attorney-at-Law with my name on my door and a staff of people to serve me.

Steinhouser notified the DDC of my response to the complaints. He felt that his credibility was also at stake here. He didn't want his integrity and reputation as an attorney to suffer because of any inconsistencies I made in my statement. He indicated to the DDC that he would be bowing out of his representation of me. He told the DDC how embarrassed I was just sitting down in front of him during our first visit. He stated that I suffered from a mental block at the time and should have told them I rejected all of her advances.

Now even my lawyer was against me. I couldn't escape the quicksand that was pulling me under.

Torn about my innocence, Steinhouser decided to offer the DDC an opportunity to take a statement from me in an attempt to keep them from going to the Inquiry Board - the next level for this investigation. He told me to tell all the facts to show I wasn't hiding something from them. He also told them not to sugarcoat anything. Any hiding of facts by me would have been fatal. He especially did not want me to exhibit any kind of anger or rage while being questioned, which was a possibility, given the turmoil I was going through. We went over the questions I might be asked concerning her advances. He told me to limit my answers as much as possible to yes and no so that I wouldn't get into more trouble.

Attorneys always instruct their clients to limit their answers to yes or no. I once prepped a client prior to his deposition and advised him to do just that. They asked him whether or not he had his foot on the brake or the gas at the time he struck the vehicle in front of him. This called for a simple one word answer, "brake or gas." Sure enough, he went into a long dissertation that he was drinking a milkshake which fell while he was driving. When he bent down to pick it up he struck the vehicle in front of him. He should have kept his mouth shut and just said brake or gas.

On this day, I wasn't the tough, thick-skinned, arrogant attorney I usually was. I was an ordinary mope who got his tit caught in the proverbial ringer. On our long, slow walk to the DDC's office, Steinhouser attempted to relax me as much as possible. As I sat in the DDC's reception room, many thoughts raced through my mind. After the Court Reporter prepared herself and her machine, we proceeded. I was sworn in by the DDC attorney and my free fall began.

Chapter 5

HOW THE ARMY CREATED A LAWYER

The day before I graduated college, the United States Army ordered me to report to the bus station in New Jersey for the long bus trip to Fort Leonard Wood, Missouri. I had 36 hours to get there. I enlisted in the Army Reserves because I didn't want to get drafted. Six months in the military sounded a hell of a lot more doable than four years.

There were about 50 of us on the bus. Some of them were gas station attendants, hamburger flippers, luggage handlers and limousine drivers. Most were guys from small towns who were molded, shaped and educated by their community's values and way of life. I may have been the only college graduate on the bus. I didn't feel I was better than them but I felt a little out of place because they seemed to look at me a little differently. Or maybe it was because I was the shortest guy on the bus.

We were met at the depot by drill sergeants who immediately had us do sit-ups and push-ups. They screamed that we were horse manure and they were going to make soldiers out of us. This wasn't jail, but it seemed to be the next worst thing. We were hauled off to the Army Base and within hours, we were brought to a square lined with stones and pebbles. A sergeant got on a large box and asked if there were any college grads in the group. There must have been 300 of us standing there. Like a dummy, me and three other guys raised our hands and were told in front of everyone that we'd be doing KP for the next six months. "We don't honor your graduate degrees in the United States Army," he shouted. "This is the military of hard knocks and now you will learn what life is all about!"

The army wasn't built for short people. I was told to drive a guy to the hospital, but I couldn't reach the Jeep's pedals. I couldn't see out of the foxhole and I couldn't shoot out of it either because it's built for six footers. "Walters," one drill sergeant told me, "you've already cut three men with your bayonet, because you're shorter than them and they're behind you marching. This must stop or they're going to kill you." My face would be black and blue because I couldn't reach the trigger housing. I had to place the stock of the rifle on the top of my shoulder instead of inside my shoulder and the rifle's backlash went into my face. My feet were always bruised because I wasn't allowed to cut off the bottom of my trousers which were far too long. I had to stuff them in the boots and it's extremely uncomfortable to march like that.

I became very sick at one point. My face blew up like a balloon when a spider bit me, but I wasn't allowed to go to Sick

Call. I didn't know what to do so I called the Rabbi. When I first entered the military this Rabbi told me that Jews were treated differently and I should be prepared for some subtle and not-so-subtle forms of persecution. For example, we weren't going to be allowed to go to services on Saturday and the Army was going to do everything they could to prevent us from doing so. Of course, that would mean more to a religious Jew that it would be to a non-practicing Jew like me. But he made it clear that I should question any orders I was given that smacked of non-preferential treatment.

The Rabbi surrounded the barracks with MP's and I was brought out and taken to the hospital. He probably saved my life. The guy on one side of me in the hospital had trench foot and they took his toes off. That was a common occurrence in the military back then. The guy on the other side of me had a hole in his neck bigger than a golf ball. The surgeon said I had a very serious infection in my nasal cavity and they needed to operate. "Once it gets in that cavity it goes into your brain and you die," he said. I said, "You're not touching me," and he asked why. "Look what you did to the patient on the right and look what you did to the one on the left," I said. Those poor saps would rue the day they went into the Army. Fortunately, I wouldn't.

The hospital treated me with massive doses of penicillin, which was unusual. They didn't want me to feel the shot so they'd slap one cheek of my ass and then slap the other one three or four times like they were playing the bongos. Then they would just jam the needle into one of my cheeks and give me the shot. I left the hospital after two weeks. No one from my family contacted me although they may not have known I was there. They knew I was in the military but it was a topic that no one talked about in our house.

When I got to the door of the hospital to be discharged, I was put into handcuffs and charged with Article 17, which the military considers to be about three steps short of treason. As punishment, I had to paint barns in small towns near the fort while handcuffed to another man. We climbed our ladders handcuffed to each other. I don't think the Army cared if we lived or died doing that. If you have a problem with absolute obedience, the Army has an even bigger problem with you. They know they're going to break you sooner or later, dead or alive. After my punishment, they put me out in a bivouac area 60 or 70 miles from the fort to guard a little supply depot. The depot had no food and they didn't give me any food supplies. For six days I had to scrounge for food and water until a Major got wind of it and sent out a whole battalion to see if I had died or deserted.

My Commanding Officer told me he better get me out of there before my six months turned into 18 months. Because I had a college degree, I could get out of the military if I went back to school. The only college that was open was a law school and classes started in 48 hours. I had to hitchhike to an airport where I could fly military standby. I made it there even though the person I was hitchhiking with had a very bad accident. He was taken by helicopter to the hospital but I didn't have a scratch on me. Luck was with me that day.

I always thought that my Army days were the worse experiences I ever had. That was where I personally faced discrimination and anti-semitism. When I was standing in that square with 300 new recruits on my first day in the Army, a Sergeant got on a big wooden box with a megaphone in his hand. I thought he'd say, Welcome to the United States Army. Instead, he asked, "Do we have any Jews here?" I knew better than to raise my hand. As bad as those military days were, they were nothing compared to the problem I was facing now.

Chapter 6

———————————————

BEING INVESTIGATED

Steinhouser's second letter of explanation was rejected. He was notified they were moving ahead and turning this matter over to the Inquiry Board, a panel of two attorneys and one non-lawyer. The panel's decisions required a simple majority which, in this case, was two votes. The Inquiry Board conducts its investigation and hears from witnesses to help it determine whether or not the charge or conduct has merit. If they find merit, they can refer this matter to the Hearing Board. I would be notified of each step in the process by my attorney. How they conduct their business is their own little secret.

Many months went by and witnesses I was unaware of appeared before the Inquiry Board. They determined that the matter was serious enough to go to a Hearing Board and voted a Formal Complaint against me.

Now began the investigation - the discovery process - much of which came from taking depositions. I was asked when I was licensed, in what state, what my practice consisted of, my hourly rate, what I charged for uncontested divorces, and so on. We both had a copy of my file and they allowed me to look at it when I couldn't remember the specifics to some of their questions. This was another fishing expedition. They wanted to learn how my law firm operated, the sequence of taking in a new client, the memos that we would dictate and why, the billing procedures, and the records that were kept. From that, they could formulate questions that would fit in with the accusations about my conduct. Most of the other questions centered around my involvement with the client who brought this action against me.

This particular Sworn Statement took three hours and had to be continued to another date. That gave the DCC the time to formulate the kind of questions they needed to "nail me." Since that time, a policy has been adopted that limits depositions to three hours. The change came too late to help me.

Steinhouser and I talked for an hour on what questions might be asked. He drilled me on the more specific allegations that she made and exactly what happened in that initial conference with her. We went over how I would answer the questions. He concentrated on the form of the answer but he never told me what to say. He wanted me to keep my answers short rather than giving them a great deal of information, some of which would only hurt me. Keep it short is a good mantra if you're testifying.

The second session took place a week later. This time they asked me questions like: Did I direct the filing of her Petition for Dissolution? Did I file a Restraining Order against her husband and, if so, when and why? When did I take over the direction and control of the case? What was discussed each time I met with her? We talked about her denial of visitation to her husband, her reconciliation with him, and her switching lawyers. Then I was asked about my belief that the maintenance her husband was offering was inadequate. I told them that she went ahead with the settlement in spite of what I recommended in person and in writing. Up until now there were no problems. It was all simple pat answers as to what actually took place.

I was asked about her advances that had been outlined in Steinhouser's second letter to the DDC. I was asked why I hadn't mentioned them in my attorney's first response. They wanted to know all the details of my appointments with her; the day, the time, where they took place and how long they lasted. I told them I had appointments with her on Saturdays and once on a Sunday. I couldn't remember how many appointments there were in total.

I told them I never met with Afshan outside of the offices. "Staying up late at night was not something I did or could do. I needed to be asleep by 8:00 p.m. so I could get up at 4:00 a.m. to work out." I went on to explain that physical exercise was necessary because of my back problem and my diabetes. I never drove her home. She once invited me to her house and I refused. I never invited her into the office for sexual purposes. I never had intercourse with her, and never attempted to. Any sexual advances were by her, all of which were emphatically rebuffed by me. All of the letters I wrote to her were professional and had to do with her case and nothing else.

I told them I knew she was flirting with me at our first appointment. Asked about family photos, I said I had never removed them from my desk or credenza because I've never tried to hide my family from anyone. I told the Board she came around my desk and put her hand on my shoulder five or six times. I never had similar contact with any other clients. I usually close my office door for privacy when I'm with clients, whether they're male or female. I believe staff interruptions make my firm look bad. On several occasions, I've even locked the door. Clients want complete privacy and are bothered by people walking in or out of my office. Confidentiality between attorney and client is sacrosanct.

They asked me if I removed her clothing or unbuttoned her blouse. They wanted to know if I fondled her genital areas and if she fondled mine. They asked me if I told her that my wife no longer turned me on. I told them I never said that and that I never touched Afshan's body. She had testified that I removed my shirt one time to avoid getting lipstick on it. It was all a lie.

They tried to show my ultimate goal was to have intercourse, but it would have been impossible to do that in my office during the day. It never happened. At no time did I ever move her hand towards my body. Contrary to what she said, I did not keep condoms in my office or my suit pocket.

After an hour and a half of questioning, we took a 30-minute break. I had coffee with my attorney in the lobby of the building and we engaged in small talk. He thought my answers were all plausible, but I didn't want to talk about the questions yet to come.

When the proceedings continued, they asked me about Afshan's demanding nature and the type of person she was. I said she was very mentally abusive when it came to billing and frequently showed up without an appointment. She left messages on my answering machine late at night and none of them were ever urgent. I made it clear that I never compromised the legality and professionalism of the case.

I was aware that her husband had a criminal battery conviction that had been expunged from his record. She told me she was physically afraid of her husband and I was aware of her safety concerns. I had no reason to disbelieve her claims of spousal brutality but I had no confirmation that they did occur. There was no question in my mind that she exhibited the pattern of a physically battered woman. I stated that I had no evidence that the husband had ever touched the children. They asked hundreds of questions regarding the battery that he committed upon her. They zeroed in on what knowledge I had and at what point I had the knowledge. The DDC attorney was trying to establish that someone in my office other than me had prepared the Order or Protection from the physical abuse. If it wasn't me, they speculated that I might have had a different interest in her situation, a sexual interest.

The DDC attorney had never practiced law in any field. She apparently went to work for the DDC right out of law school. Most DDC attorneys have had no practical experience in any field of law. They have no clue how an office operates. I tried to establish with them that I remained in the office and did less of the courtroom work than my staff attorneys. When they were in court, I would see the new clients and answer the calls of their other clients.

The DDC attorney didn't care about my answers. She needed to believe that I was taking advantage of my client because the difficult and stressful situations in her life made her quite vulnerable. Because of that, all of the questions seemed to be aimed at coming up with anything that could possibly label me as a sex maniac. The DDC attorney tried to establish that my client was abused and had a difficult time in separating from her husband. They questioned me about his staying out late at night, drinking and watching belly dancers at local taverns. They also returned to the many occasions when I said she had turned up unannounced and caused a ruckus. I told them that the lawyer who represented her before she came to me was working on a Chancery case with her. He had settled the case when she pulled the rug out from under him without his knowledge and against his advice and recommendations.

Then they caught me completely off guard. They referenced a letter I had sent Afshan in August and asked me if I had prepared it. I told them I did but I couldn't remember why I sent it. She had reconciled with her husband for a second time and the letter indicated that I was cancelling her bill. "I can only speculate she called me about the bills she was still getting," I responded. "I told her I was cancelling her bill." The bill was a very small amount.

They wanted to know each time I met with her, the reasons why and the hours on those particular days. They were looking for late evening hours when no one was around to help them prove that I intended to be with her sexually. This line of questioning lasted more than 45 minutes. They gave me times and dates and asked if I was there with her and whether we were alone. They asked who was in the office, which office we met in, if the door was closed and locked and at whose request the meetings were made. They asked if I had any follow-up correspondence to the meetings and what took place in these meetings. Because an "a" had inadvertently been added to the end of her name in one of the letters, they asked if I had a pet name for her.

They went over my billings item by item, date by date, to discern what I did and what I didn't do for her. They wanted to establish that our relationship was more of a sexual nature than it was anything else. They wanted to claim that everything I did was a "form of endearment" even though it was not. Their goal was to prove false my theory that she seduced me.

I knew that the DDC was trying to establish that the story I had given Steinhouser was pure fiction. I told them I was embarrassed for not mentioning her advances, especially the one on that Sunday morning. I said I was embarrassed for having her come in on a Sunday and not telling the DDC about it. "At no time did I ever go to a hotel or motel with her. At no time did I ever have intercourse with her. At no time did I call her into the office for the purpose of having sexual contact. At no time did I ever compromise her legal situation." I said this as firmly as I could without appearing to be desperate.

I explained how in June or July of that year, she came to my office late one morning without an appointment and demanded to see me. There were several people in the waiting room who had appointments. I had to come out to find out about the disturbance and she started demanding through the Reception Room window that she HAD to see me AT ONCE. She yelled that she could never see me when she wanted to see me and I didn't respond to her needs. My staff tried to calm her down. I was highly embarrassed by the episode.

"This file includes copies of all the letters I've written her," I said. "If my intent was anything other than a legal matter, I would not have written those letters. I would have had her come to my office. She came up with $8,000 to purchase a building yet claimed she had no money. This and other things made me skeptical about her story. Nevertheless, I always protected her legally as any good attorney would. To do anything else would be a betrayal of our ethics as attorneys."

I was as honest and contrite as I could possibly be. I poured out my soul in response to the DDC attorney's questions, but it was clear she was still pushing to make her case. If that attorney had any skepticism, it was directed solely at me and not to my client. How she managed to not question any part of my client's story was unbelievable to me. The DDC attorney was trying to establish that my accuser's integrity was unquestionable and that I had no defense for the sexual questions I was being asked. She wanted a concrete base to show that my client's allegations were far more believable than any story I might come up with.

She started asking me questions about how I felt about Afshan's physical features and if I was ever "turned on" by her. I was asked if I ever had contact of a physical or sexual nature with a divorce client. I admitted that some clients hug me when they thank me and they initiate the contact. Some clients break down and cry in front of me and I embrace them as a gesture of support. I told them I realized Afshan initially made subtle flirtatious advances towards me because she wanted to know if I was married and had any children. Once she found out I was married with children, her advances became stronger and more serious.

I was asked what I did to discourage her behavior. I said I didn't respond and she went back and sat at my desk. There were a lot of questions regarding any kissing that took place, but that's not what they were really interested in learning.

Q. Did she remove any of your clothing?
A. No.
Q. Did you touch each other anywhere on your body?
A. No.
Q. Was there any specific fondling of any genital areas of either your body or her body?
A. No.
Q. After that Sunday appointment, did you do any additional work on her case?
A. I don't recall.
Q. At any point during your representation of her, did you tell her that you found her attractive?
A. No.
Q. Did you ever say "no" to her or that you did not want to represent her in her divorce case after the first contact?

A. She's not the type of person you could say no to. She was very demeaning and very demanding.

Q. Did you ever attempt to withdraw from her representation in the Dissolution of Marriage?

A. No.

Q. You don't seem to recall what you did on specific dates. Why is that?

A. I do a volume practice of divorces and generally see 10 to 15 clients a day.

Q. Did you touch her genital area?

A. No.

Q. Never?

A. Never!

Q. Did you ever tell her that you loved her?

A. I never told her I loved her.

There were numerous questions about having oral sex with her and I'll spare you the particulars. I denied all of those allegations.

Q. Did you ever attempt to have sexual intercourse with her while she was lying on the couch in your office?

A. No.

Q. Are you sure?

A. Yes. I did not have intercourse with her!

Q. I didn't say have intercourse. Did you ever try to have sexual intercourse with her while she was laying on the couch in your office?

A. During the day? In a crowded office? With my wife no more than 50 feet from my office? That would be ludicrous. This whole thing is ludicrous!

Q. Did she ever tell you she was here for her divorce and not for a sexual relationship?

A. No.

The questions became increasingly ridiculous. Was the couch in my office cloth or leather? Was it tufted or not tufted? How wide was it? What color was it? How many cushions did it have? Did I ever spend a night sleeping on the couch in my office? This was not a question of my admitting to sexual contact, though they wanted everybody to think it was. They were trying to make new law and had chosen me as their guinea pig. They were setting me up to be the first attorney in our state, and possibly the country, to be disbarred because of consensual sexual touching with a client. Timing really is everything, and it didn't seem to be in my favor.

They asked what I thought would be the reason that motivated her to file the Complaint. I told them she filed her Complaint with the DDC the day after she stormed into my office without an appointment and demanded to see me. I said she was very irritated when I wouldn't see her. Most important, I had stressed to her that she could not get away with denying visitation of her children to her ex-husband. As much as she alleged that her husband had beaten her on several occasions, she never asked for supervised visitation.

The DDC attorney asked me if I thought the Clarence Thomas hearings where Anita Hill had testified, had anything to do with motivating her to file the Complaint with the DDC. I said I thought it did. In my defense, I told them Afshan would call me and leave messages at all hours of the night. I reluctantly return all my phone calls even if they wake me up and I'd tell her that it could wait until the next day. I stressed the need for urgency to justify her late-night calls. One time she called when she thought her husband was seeing a belly dancer in Las Vegas.

I couldn't understand why my attorney didn't object to the repetitive nature of the questions. Perhaps it was because this statement was being taken at his request so that I could recant <u>my</u> false statements, and he could distance himself from me.

After we finished, Steinhouser and I had a cup of coffee. We both agreed that the DDC attorney was not really truthful with us in taking this Sworn Statement. She was well prepared to prosecute this case no matter what I said. It was the case that was going to make her a star. It would be the first case where a lawyer would be convicted or lose his license for touching a client.

In truth, there was no sexual encounter between my client and me. No intimacy. No intercourse. She was a woman who felt scorned by me because I demanded that she give her husband visitation with their minor children. That really was the crux of this whole matter. I was being crucified because I had told the truth and tried to protect her from damaging herself. Like they say, "No good deed goes unpunished."

Chapter 7

HANDCUFFS

I went to college at a large Midwestern university and became a member of a popular fraternity. I was like a little fish in a very big pond, so it felt good to belong to something. I was in my second year when three fraternity brothers said they were going to a little town about 100 miles away where there was a network of whore houses. They had been there before, but I hadn't. I think if I had said no to going with them, they would have branded me as something less than all-man, but the idea of paying for sex never appealed to me. But, owing to that little monster every kid knows as peer pressure, me and another frat brother went with them. After all, outside of a small chance of picking up a communicable disease, what possibly could go wrong this one time?

They parked about half a block from one whore house, but when we got out of the car, they said they were going to another place a little further down the road. They asked us if we wanted to go with them, but I said, "Since we're right here, we'll go to this place. Just tell us what to do." They told us to walk through an alley and to knock on the door of the first house on the left. They figured we had enough intelligence to take it from there.

As we were walking down the center of the alley, we were surrounded by six squad cars and 10 or 12 cops with their guns drawn. They put us up against the wall, spread eagled us and kept jabbing their rifles in our gut. They told us we were under arrest for armed robbery and ordered us not to put our arms down. We had to keep them up for half an hour and that was the most painful thing I have ever experienced. I've since learned that in China they used to punish law breakers by having them kneel on uneven concrete stones for hours on end. For most people, 15 seconds is all they can take of this torture. I guess I should consider myself lucky.

They brought us into the station, emptied our pockets, and formally charged us with armed robbery. We emptied our pockets and they saw the rubbers. What they didn't see was any evidence that would indicate we had robbed anybody. Between the two of us, my friend and I had just enough money for the whore house. The only possible weapon we may have been carrying was a comb. I can see it now: "Two young University students were arrested after a crime spree where they robbed six jewelry stores holding a comb. Use of a black comb enhances the charge to a hate crime. Film at Eleven."

We were released the following day but we didn't know why. Of course, back then we weren't very savvy and had no legal experience. We were just happy to get out of there. The other guys came back and picked us up after we called them.

Later, we found out that the madam who owned the house of ill repute was not paying the cops as she normally did, and the cops were trying to teach her a lesson. We thought it was the end of the matter.

Right before the next semester's final exams, the university called us and said they knew about the arrest, knew that we spent a night a jail and knew that we had been charged with armed robbery. They were in the process of expelling us from school. Maybe some students could concentrate on their finals in such a situation, but I certainly could not. I passed my exams with a D-. Well, that was the last we heard from the school and nothing ever happened. We weren't about to call the school and say "Hey, you forget to expel us," so we just let it slide.

Two weeks before the next semester's final exams, the school called and said they forgot to expel us. The original paperwork had been eaten by the dean's dog and this time they were going to do it for sure! Well, nothing happened for another two or three semesters. I was still in the university when I got a call from the city attorney who said he wanted us to come in and sign releases, guaranteeing that we weren't going to sue the city for false arrest.

My brother was a young attorney at the time and I asked him to fly in so he could go with us. He said we should sign the release, although I don't know why. We had a very good case, and the City knew it. I've always had a nagging feeling we shouldn't have signed it. Of course, he did prevent us from being exposed or embarrassed, but I'm pretty sure a couple of thousand dollars would have minimized my emotional pain.

A few years later, I saw my fellow criminal walking down the street towards me. We both raised our hands up high and kept them up until we stopped each other. We did that every time we ever saw each other on the street. It was our "put your hands up" nod, the secret handshake that only we knew. My friend became a very prominent businessman and started his own very successful national chain of restaurants. One day, he asked me if I told my children about our arrest. I said yes, and he said, "I bet nobody believed it, did they?" He was right. He also said his arms still hurt after all these years. "You're a lucky guy," I told him, "because my arms are the only part of my body that doesn't hurt."

And here I was many years later, feeling like I was in jail. But this time, the cuffs were tighter.

Chapter 8

MY NEW DEFENSE

Before this matter went to a Hearing Board, Steinhouser called to say he wanted to see me immediately. He told me he had a heavy criminal defense schedule and my case had been taking up too much of his time. He thought my case would have been dismissed with the original letter, but there was the matter of the follow-up letter. He didn't expect it would go as far as a Sworn Statement being taken. He recommended I go see a well-known attorney by the name of William J. Crawford who had vast experience in DDC defenses.

I hadn't expected this and I was shocked. By God, I'm a lawyer! Why am I being treated this way, I thought to myself. I felt I was doing the right thing with the second letter which detailed that she had tried to seduce me and that I had rejected her advances. I felt that my statements would show the DDC that I wanted to be truthful. My legal representation of this woman was excellent. I got her divorced on her terms, after which her post-divorce problems caused the matter to become very contentious. Why are they making such a big thing out of this? Why is my attorney dropping me like a hot potato? Steinhouser and I shook hands and he wished me the best of luck with Crawford.

I needed to find out more about this new attorney. I pulled up some of the court files of DDC matters where Crawford was the attorney. I obtained the names of the accused lawyers he represented and called some of them when I got back to my office. I got glowing reviews about Crawford as a result of my efforts.

In legal cases, a win is not as important as working out a good outcome. Sometimes you just can't win, but you can keep the damages to a minimum. In my case, it was a matter of keeping my license to practice law, so I made an appointment with Crawford. He told me of his vast experience in DDC matters, but admitted he was booked solid and probably could not represent me at this time. It was his experience that because I initially denied everything, I was facing a very difficult, uphill battle. Crawford thought that Steinhouser's defense theory that I was seduced and that the woman was lying was a proper tactic. He recommended his associate, Ron Woodhouse, who had handled hundreds of DDC defense matters and did a lot of Crawford's work when Crawford's calendar was overloaded. He walked me over to Woodhouse's office which was about 20 feet down the hall.

I told Woodhouse that there was no way I should be disbarred over this matter. We both understood this case was the first of its kind in the state of New York and agreed I was going to be the guinea pig. Woodhouse was down to earth and he understood me and my predicament. We hit it off very well.

We both agreed that the DDC attorney wanted to make a name for herself and needed all the publicity that she could get. It was now his job to stop this matter from going to a Hearing Board where they have a right to vote a Formal Complaint. What we didn't know, and that included Steinhouser, was that a major stumbling block was about to appear in front of me.

Woodhouse immediately advised the DDC that he would be representing me now. He wrote a very detailed, highly convincing correspondence which pointed out that my accuser was not entirely credible and quite erratic. He cited the fact that she acknowledged that her husband did not report his income in its entirety and that she signed those tax returns anyway. When a person lies once, it makes it a lot easier to lie again.

Prior to becoming my firm's client, she had retained another lawyer in connection with an $8,000 loan she made to her sister and brother-in-law. They had borrowed money from her and promised to put her name on the title to the property they were buying. When they failed to keep their word, her lawyer filed a lawsuit. Later, the brother-in-law convinced her that they would pay her. She fired that lawyer, apparently against all advice. She then changed her mind and sought my help. I had agreed to file a Motion for her and once again she changed her mind and refused to follow my recommendations. I had her write a document in her own handwriting stating that she was refusing to follow my advice and wanted me to withdraw the Motion. Despite this, she later blamed me and my firm for not adequately representing her.

She also stated that she was not fully advised about the support agreement. However, the bill she received from me indicated that I had sent her a letter advising her that she shouldn't proceed with the divorce until she obtained a job because she was to receive alimony for only six months. She refused my advice, just as she had ignored the advice of her previous attorney. She had a pattern of not following legal advice, and would get mad and fire her lawyers when they admonished her. The lawyers became her enemy. In her mind, I was Public Enemy #1.

Woodhouse's letter on my behalf stated that Afshan consistently complained about how badly her husband treated her, yet she reconciled with him while I was handling her divorce. Later, her husband allegedly mistreated her again and I was required to seek an Order of Protection. They reconciled again, but then had another falling out. Woodhouse claimed this was a love/hate relationship with her husband and that she seemed to have transferred her mixed feelings onto me. I thought it was an excellent interpretation of the psychological problems she was going through.

I had told Afshan that denying her husband visitation to punish him was actually punishing the children. Woodhouse said her judgment regarding the welfare of her children was clouded by her ambivalent and often violent attitude toward her ex-husband. Woodhouse said her descriptions of what occurred with me were frequently inspired by the DDC's questionnaire. When prompted, she became more graphic but she insisted that what sexual contact occurred was absolutely abhorred by her, even though she told no one about it and kept returning to my office. Hers were the emotional statements of a person who always perceives herself as the victim.

She said she frequently demanded to see me when she came into the office. I preferred to write to her instead of her coming into the office because of the constant confrontations. Of course, I never spoke to her other than in a professional capacity on the phone. Woodhouse concluded this portion of the letter by stating it was her intent, not mine, to have a sexual relationship. He backed up my integrity as a lawyer and stated that my firm has many associates and four secretaries, all of whom had families relying on my firm's continued operation. He asserted that my firm had hundreds of divorce clients of modest means who have paid hard earned money towards their divorces. To demonstrate my good faith, he spoke of my commitment to handle three to five pro bono divorce cases, averaging 25 to 45 hours of work each year.

Woodhouse maintained that the magnitude of the effect on my family, weighed against the incident in question, was certainly out of balance. "There is no case law preventing sexual contact with clients by lawyers," said Woodhouse. "Cases in other jurisdictions cite the conflict of interest problems which may arise but, in this case, there was certainly no negative impact on her legal representation."

He then got into the specifics of the sexual contact. Both my accuser and I agreed that there was no sexual intercourse. At no time did I take her to a hotel, visit her at home, or attempt to establish a relationship with her. She never complained of getting unwanted phone calls during the day or at night. We never

66

went out socially. Woodhouse recognized the nature of the "she said, he said" allegations. He emphasized that my integrity had been placed on the "back burner" while my client's seductive advances had been ignored by the DDC. He suggested that a private letter of admonishment would serve both the profession and me. If similar conduct were ever leveled against me, the case could be re-opened. I thought his letter was a masterpiece. I certainly could not have written a better one.

Chapter 9

THEY'RE COMING OUT OF THE WOODWORK

To my dismay, the Hearing Board voted a formal complaint. I kind of thought the fix was in because this little case was one that everybody seemed to want to litigate. For the life of me, I couldn't understand why. Notices to produce my documents and my file would be issued. Subpoenas would be issued to witnesses they thought would be unfavorable to me, along with other witnesses they knew would be favorable to their case. Major litigation was now afoot.

How did this matter get out of hand? Why is this happening? Why is it that *my* statements have so little credibility and *hers* are accepted as fact? If I had $5 for every time I thought about this, I could retire and live off the interest.

Woodhouse's letter was terrific but neither of us knew he was fighting a battle on numerous fronts. We didn't know that the DDC had done an extensive investigation and had pulled the names of hundreds of my files from the last few years. I also didn't know they had contacted my current and former employees. Using leading questions, they convinced a few former clients to state that I had made sexual advances towards them. I was upset that Steinhouser didn't tell me they had this information and that this type of an investigation was going on.

I was shocked when I read a letter from one of my employees who had responded to the DDC inquiry. Helena Rojas worked as a secretary in my office for about a year and was fired two weeks prior to her conversation with the DDC. She told them on her last day of work I offered her $5,000. She was unclear as to the purpose of the money but she said she told me to give her the paycheck so she could go. She said I made her first two months at the firm torture, harassing her every day by telling her how nice she looked. She claimed I would ask her to dinner and dancing, though anyone who knows me will tell you that neither of those things was my cup of tea. She said I told her I wasn't married and there was no obstruction to prevent us from seeing each other. Everything she said was totally untrue. My wife worked in the office a couple of days a week so everybody in the office knew her and knew we were married.

After a couple of supposed indiscretions on my part, Helena stated that she asked me not to bother her and talk to her in "that way." She said it was like talking to a brick wall. Come to think of it, maybe she was talking to a brick wall because she never said that to me. After two months I supposedly asked her to switch from divorce work to personal injury work because I thought she wasn't doing a good job. She said the harassment from me started up again after another couple of months. She said I came over to her desk and sang lyrics like, "Don't forsake me, oh my darling." She said I decreased her salary by more than $50 per week.

I have never lowered an employee's salary in all the years I've practiced law, a fact that I could easily prove. This conversation from my past employee was false and bordered on the idiotic. I have no idea why she made these statements, even if the DDC had led her down the path of sexual involvement they had me on.

The DDC inappropriately advised her that I was charged with a conflict of interest for engaging in a sexual relationship with one of my clients. They encouraged the woman to say that I made sexual advances towards her. She said I showed her photographs of people's private parts and that she just ignored my behavior. No such allegations of sexual impropriety had surfaced from her until the DDC told her that was why they had brought charges against me.

It's one thing to assume I'm guilty, but it's quite another thing for the DDC to tell people that they truly believe I am. They're setting up grounds for an appeal, but appeals only take place after a decision has been rendered. It was as if the attorney for the DDC wanted me to spend as much of my money defending myself as I possibly could.

How could the DDC have an unbiased attitude towards me in view of all the crazies who are only too happy to come out of the woodwork? Why the hell is the DDC telling people such serious allegations against me when all they have are allegations? I just didn't understand how Steinhouser could have been aware of these incidents before we sent a reply to the Complaint. Why the hell did he allow this? Sometimes, truth really is the first casualty.

The DDC also produced the transcript of a phone conversation during which a woman complained that her attorney and myself were involved in a 'conspiracy' and were colluding with each other. This is a common complaint among clients when things don't go the way they want them to go. The DDC noted that she had nothing to substantiate her claims and advised the woman they didn't have any specific or substantial charges from this conversation to assist them. Thank God I didn't have to respond to the claims of a second unhappy, untruthful client.

There were notes from another telephone call when a client advised the DDC that I had represented her husband in a divorce with another party. She complained I met with the Judge and opposing counsel in the Judge's chambers, but refused to tell her what was discussed. This, too, was a complete fabrication. No lawyer would ever refuse to tell their clients what was going on after a pre-trial conference with the opposing counsel in the Judge's chambers.

Even Judges get numerous complaints from clients who claim that the Judge made sexual advances towards them. That's why new rules are now in place to prevent attorneys from bringing their clients into the chambers for pre-trial conference with the Judge and opposing counsel. Too many allegations have been made by clients against Judges that were ludicrous and false, but had to be investigated seriously.

Chapter 10

NO DRAPES IN
THE OFFICE

I didn't know that Afshan had given a Sworn Statement to the DDC. My attorney wasn't present when the Statement was given so they had a battery of information to help them formulate their questions prior to my Sworn Statement. Afshan laid it on pretty thick, that's for sure.

She said she was hurt and depressed when she came to see me. Her heart was broken. She claimed that the first time I saw her I looked at her in a way that indicated that I liked her. She said I started to stare at her and that I was always "looking at her," particularly at her breasts and her "behind." Her initial intake was with me and after that she saw my associate, Mr. Grant. She said after that meeting, I told Mr. Grant I would take over her case. This was not true and Mr. Grant could substantiate my denial.

Throughout Afshan's entire statement, the DDC attorney was asking her questions like, "He looked at you in a flirtatious manner, didn't he?" or, "He constantly stared at you as if he wanted you?" The DDC attorney was helping her build the case against me. They let her expound on how she turned to God and the Bible for strength to withstand my behavior. Like I said, she laid it on pretty damn thick. She said her father was a priest and she believed in Jesus Christ. She didn't know who she could turn to so she went to a priest and told him everything. She was so embarrassed that she begged the priest not to tell anybody in the Church.

She couldn't remember how many times she met with me, but guessed it was four or five. She continued to maintain that I would only see her for late afternoon or early evening appointments, in spite of her continuing protests. She said I would lock the door after she came into my office and asked me, "Why are you locking your door?" She claimed I said, "Because we're closed." She said it was fine, but only because she wanted to see what I was going to do. She felt something was wrong when she came into my office because I immediately "came after her." She claimed I said I liked her very much from the first day I saw her, that I wanted more time with her and that I told her she was attractive, beautiful, had great eyes, and was very sexy. She said she was extremely shocked by all of this.

"Don't worry," I supposedly told her. "We have time and I'll take care of your case. I like you very much. You're a very beautiful woman." She said she was sitting in a chair at the time and I was standing very close to her. She said she couldn't move from her chair and I repeated the compliments I paid her.

''Here I'm going through a divorce and I was already very hurt from my ex-husband, I was tied up financially. It's not the time to hear those words. It wasn't in my dreams. He said those things to me. It's like you go for help and medicine and they give you poison instead. I said, I'm not looking for a relationship. I need your help. I have two children.

"He pulled out a Kleenex and told me to wipe off my lipstick. I asked why. He said because I want to kiss you. I pushed him and said, don't do this. I wanted to get up from the chair but he held me down. I didn't know what to do. I wanted to leave."

The DDC attorney asked her, "He held you in his arms tight?" She answered by saying, "He moved his right hand on my back and the other hand was holding me. He started kissing me around the face and on the lips. He held me strong. I felt trapped. He kissed me around the neck. On the lips. I felt frozen. I said, are you married? Do you do this to all your clients? He said, no, I never did it to anyone except you. He said he loves me. He said that more than ten times. I said I felt hurt that my husband had betrayed me." She claimed that all this took place on her first appointment with me.

She blamed her failed attempts at marital reconciliation on me. She said her husband knew that somebody was trying to get her to be unfaithful to him, their marriage, and their God. He could tell just by looking at her and she said that made her unclean in his eyes. Her message was that all men were animals first and everything else second. All I could think while I was reading the transcript was that her true calling in life was to write trashy romance novels. Oh, what a web this woman could weave.

Afshan said every time I made an advance, she told me she wasn't interested. "I didn't feel anything. It was like touching the table. I pushed him away many times. He was trying to kiss me and he put his hand on my chest. He finally let me go. I'm not here for this, I told him. He didn't work on my divorce case, not even for five minutes. He would rush close to me as I was trying to open the door and leave. He held my hand talking to me. I would say, please, please don't touch me. He worked a little bit on my case. Most of my appointments with him would be on Saturdays and he saw me every week, sometimes every two weeks, sometimes three times a week. I'm not exactly sure.

"He held my hand and pulled my hand this way and that way. He put my hand over my crotch and I was embarrassed, felt trapped, and was very hurt. He was fully clothed and he started pulling down my zipper. I was so embarrassed. I didn't tell my priest what happened because of that. He pulled out his penis, grabbed my wrist roughly and made me touch him. I felt sick and disgusted. It made him feel good. He said, I'm in love with you sweetheart. I love you honey."

Afshan testified under oath that I ejaculated quickly, then said I ejaculated into a condom. She didn't say, nor was she asked, if there were two different incidents. If there were only one condom incident, how could she have two different versions of it? It's as if the DDC had given my client carte blanche when it came to accusing me.

At this point the DDC attorney asked my client if she needed some water or a moment to compose herself. Seriously? Don't moments like that only happen in movies? All of the DDC's leading questions were answered by her in broken English. There were no questions like, what did he do next? Instead, the questions were, "He did A, B and C next and you didn't like it, did you?" Every question was prompting her every answer, as had been rehearsed. While listening to this fiction I wondered why she didn't fire me if I did everything she said I did? Why did she keep coming back? Why was my attorney silent? What planet am I on?

The DDC was making the case they wanted to make. They didn't care if they were being fair to me or even conducting themselves in an ethical fashion. They wanted to make new law and that's where they were going with this witch hunt. They were looking to disbar me and I couldn't let them succeed. They decided on their position and then worked backwards to justify it. You see, mine was the case on which they would "make their bones," and they would do anything and everything to build their case. They had taken a faulty first premise and built the foundation of their house around it. The fact that they had built it on sand didn't seem to bother them in the least. I've always considered that to be intellectual dishonesty at its worst, not to mention an egregious abuse of power.

When Afshan continued her testimony the questions produced more graphic responses. "The door was locked," she said. "He come up to my face, would hold me in his arms and squeeze me so hard to his chest. This is why I could not move. Many times I pushed him."

Q. He fondled your breast, didn't he?
A. He used to touch me on the breast. He asked to remove my clothing. It happened on the second appointment.

Q. Did you ever think of going to a new lawyer?

A. I could not afford another lawyer. I already paid him $750. I felt he stole my money. I borrowed the money from my brother-in-law. I felt hurt, trapped, the money was not mine. I borrowed it. (I'm sitting there wondering why she never asked for her money back. Not to mention that $350 of the $750 went toward Court costs.) The third appointment I said, Look, I'm not here for anything what you think. I'm not here. I don't feel. I love my husband. He said he understood. He would come close to me, slap me on the back and say, I understand how you feel. He would slap my back and say, "Don't worry about money. I'll give you whatever you want. As much as you need. Just be with me."

Q. He referred to you sexually?

A. I don't sell my body. I'm a Christian. At the third appointment, we were standing and holding hands. I said, 'I'm not a whore. I don't sell myself.' I pushed my hand down from his grabbing my hands and sat down before he could hug me. He closed the door and said, 'Tell me, I love you.' He said, 'I love you' and he held my face. I said, I don't love you. I hired you as an attorney.' He said, 'Goddammit, I've got to have you!' He repeated this, Goddammit, many times. He held my wrist towards his penis. He pulled the zipper down again. My hand touched it. He ejaculated again. He grabbed a tissue to clean it up. It was like a nightmare. He was out of control. He open my blouse and tell me what beautiful breasts I had. He kissed my breasts. I wore a brassiere. It was a half cup bra. I would be pushing him away when he was doing this. He would hold me against the wall and pull my skirt or dress to feel my legs. Then he sat on the table and started talking about my case. He has a table in addition to his desk. He has drawn drapes, and he draws the drapes when I come in.

(I don't have drapes in my office. I have blinds. I've never said the word Goddammit in my life. And, doesn't the fact that she mentioned she was wearing a half cup bra bring her credibility and truthfulness into question just a tiny little bit? It didn't.)

She culminated her answers by saying I had ejaculated all over her and her clothes. But she also said we never went to a motel, reservations were never made to anywhere, that I never took her to a restaurant, that I did give her a ride home on one occasion, but that I never came into her house and that I actually dropped her off a block away from her home. It was as if she was supplementing the facts of the case with facts of her own. I knew I had absolutely no control over what people thought, or what they were told to think. I know this will sound harsh, but my client and the people at the DDC were trying to ruin my life for reasons that had nothing to do me.

It was now clear that my success would come down to questions from my attorney that would bring out a possible motive as to why she was lying. She said that I always took her husband's side more than hers. She claimed the reason I couldn't get any more money for her was because her husband had a cash business that allowed him to hide his money. She then claimed that she didn't go back to my firm because I never helped her. She didn't say she didn't go back to me because there were sexual encounters, only because I never helped her. My files and the files of my associates would clearly indicate otherwise.

Then she laid into her husband, who, unlike me, deserved the treatment. "I still love my husband," she said. "I found pictures of my ex-husband with other women. He used to tell me how much he loves me. I also wanted the lawyer to ask for more child support but he didn't pay any attention to me. My husband spent $10,000 on belly dancers. Here are some photos I'm showing you. I think he's a dog." So, she still loves her husband but she's thinks he's a dog. Afshan was obviously out of control at this point but the DDC attorney did everything she could to calm her down.

"I called here and someone suggested I see a priest," said Afshan. "The next day I saw a priest. Then I sent a letter to you. I confessed everything to my priest. The priest said, don't call him back. I called the lawyer and he asked why I called. I told him I want to see him. He said, can you make it today? Now? I said. Why? Why should I come there today?"

The questions became increasingly redundant. Their thinking seemed to be that if you repeat something enough times, it becomes true by default. Norman Mailer called that a factoid. I think a jury would have seen right through the shenanigans of the DDC attorney. She should have asked questions like, "If your finances were so bad, why didn't you go to a free legal clinic? Why did you dress so provocatively when you came to his office? Why did you wear a half cup brassiere?" Of course, my attorney would have asked these questions of her if he had been notified of the deposition.

I was completely dismayed by Afshan's Sworn Statement and her answers. She managed to tell her story in detailed confession and in broken English, all of which went to portray me as a nut case. She was dramatic, aggressive, intimidating and very seductive. She had either embellished or made up everything that she said took place. She created some detailed sexual maneuvers in an attempt to get sympathy from anyone who cared to listen. Shouldn't she be held to at least some level of accountability here? Punish me in an appropriate way, but let's not go hog wild!

Chapter 11

WHERE IT ALL BEGAN

My father was the youngest of nine children and was the only one who was able to have children. His brothers and sisters were somewhat ostracized because of this and they left home at an early age to avoid a lifetime of humiliation. Dad was shoveling coal in his parent's house by the time he was six because there was nobody else around to do it. His father was a bartender in a bar he co-owned with a cousin. My father was rejected by the military either because of ear problems or because he was the only child left to support his mother.

Dad sold life insurance in his younger days. He was a real good looking man when he met my mother. She was a controlling individual and came from a well to do family. My mother was courted by some very well known people in the city of New York including the Feingolds, one of whom owned a bank and one of whom had a hospital pavilion named after him. He proposed to my mother before my father came along but she turned him down. She knew what she wanted and she always won. My

father had no college education and I don't think he ever graduated from high school, but he was a very good life insurance
salesman and a sweet person who won her heart.

My mother convinced him to work for her father in the
plumbing supply business. My father had no knowledge of
plumbing supplies or equipment and was hired on an unusual
basis. If he needed money he would ask for it but he wouldn't
receive a salary. This was also true of my uncle who was my
grandfather's son. My uncle was the favorite and we were
sure he received money under the table. And what did my
father get? He was ridiculed by his father-in-law, controlled
by his father-in-law, controlled by my uncle and controlled
by his wife.

Ralph Walters was a simple man with little formal education. On the weekends my mother would dress him up like a
king. She would buy expensive suits and sport jackets for him
even though his daily work clothes were those of a blue collar
worker. My mother's friends were a mixture of suits who had
good jobs as professionals or owned businesses. My mother was
the controlling factor for many of her friends and whatever my
mother did, they followed. She got more satisfaction from this
than from any other part of her life.

My father wasn't a plumber, but since he was selling to
plumbers, he had to know what they were doing. His crash-
course in the business took place under the critical eyes of my
grandfather. The old man worked in the store and lived on the
floor above it. My father was told to eat his lunch upstairs which
he did for a few years. He finally went out to eat his meals at a

restaurant like my uncle had been doing all along. Turns out that dad's jail cell was closed, but it wasn't locked.

My grandfather was a very unusual person. Except for his business, he was a recluse if there ever was one. He never left his own street unless there was a funeral to attend. He had a driver's license, but kept his car in the backyard. Nobody cut the grass and the weeds ended up camouflaging the car so well that no one ever knew it was there. I recall it was a 1948 Chevy four-door sedan.

My grandfather lived upstairs of the store but he kept monkey wrenches, screwdrivers and pliers in the refrigerator. He wasn't the neatest man in the world but he liked his tools cold. He invested his money wisely and owned a little piece of property with six or seven major investors. Over time, they came to have holdings in real estate throughout the City of New York and my grandfather had maybe half a percent or one percent of each parcel. He never changed his clothes and always wore a suit to work. It was an odd way to dress because a plumbing store was all dirt, dust and grease. Clothes were not a line item in his budget. He carried pipe to the trucks. My grandmother was 5'3" and she loaded and unloaded trucks as well. In the back of the store was an office, consisting of three desks and chairs. My grandmother had a very little kitchen next to the coal-fired furnace. She had a refrigerator and a table and as a young kid I would go to the back of the store and she'd cook me hamburgers there, instead of going upstairs to the kitchen.

My uncle treated my father like a dog and had no respect for him at all. Ironically, my uncle was a very gregarious person who treated me with respect. As I grew up he also treated my kids with respect. But he had demons in his life. His first son was born with Dystonia which is like MS in that the mind is not affected but the body is. I became very attached to his son and we grew close. As time progressed, my aunt tried to convince him to commit suicide. She felt there was no life for him with this disease as he was becoming increasingly trapped inside a body that wouldn't let him speak. Many times I got calls from the hospital to tell me that he was having his stomach pumped and the only person they could call was me. They couldn't call his mom because she was the person who encouraged him to commit suicide. When my aunt learned that I had gone to the hospital to bail him out, so to speak, she didn't speak to me for months.

At one time I did try to track down some of my father's siblings but it wasn't easy. I found one in a flophouse on Clark Street in Chicago so I flew there to visit him. He was very polite and told me he put his teeth back in his mouth just before I arrived. He lived in a room no bigger than a small bathroom, with a bed, a little chair to hold his belongings, and a very small television. He did have a job at one time but apparently was retired when I saw him. He died a couple of years later, but my father died before him. I called him on the phone in the hall of the flophouse. I told him the funeral was in New York and that I would pay his airfare. He wasn't interested in coming to the funeral nor was he interested in seeing my father even in his casket. I never talked to him after that and I learned he was buried as an unknown person in an unmarked grave.

I found another one of my father's siblings in Las Vegas. For some reason, everyone in the family thought she was gay, but I found her happily married to a guy. That was the only time I ever saw her. She may have been the only one on my dad's side siblings who found love. I hope that wasn't the case but it wouldn't surprise me if it were.

Chapter 12

THERAPY

When I first saw Woodhouse, he told me he needed to show **the court** that I was making a good faith attempt to become a better person. I knew he was telling me that he had to show I wasn't a risk to society. It would help him if he had some backup medical testimony at the hearing from a psychiatrist.

Whoever I saw would have to testify and the results had better be in my favor. I had never been to a psychiatrist in my life. I knew a psychiatrist who worked out at my health club and decided to see him. I told him I needed somebody to testify on my behalf, but I didn't ask him for a favorable diagnosis before we started. After talking it over with others, he decided not to see me. I'm not sure why he decided that way, but I know that when you ask a friend to do you a favor, they're probably wondering if they're going to have to do it for free.

My own family physician referred me to a psychiatrist whose office was near mine. I started seeing him once a month during the DDC litigation. His small reception room had two chairs and felt like a large closet. There was a door ringer button on the wall for patients to announce their arrival. There was no secretary or windows and I felt like I was in a cage. Apparently, most psychiatrists don't have secretaries and do their own typing and communicate with their patients on the phone. The 45-minute session with a psychiatrist is very exact. They start on time and they end on time, and they have a few minutes in between patients to return any phone calls.

I arrived early and he introduced himself to me. In his office were a chair and a large couch, along with a desk and desk chair. There were no windows in his office either. His desk faced a wall so he had to turn around on his swivel chair in order to talk to me. He started a tape recorder which immediately made me uncomfortable. I was surprised by my reaction, but attributed it to the huge amount of stress I was under. We sat quietly until he turned his chair around and said, "Well."

I started from the beginning and told him everything about my upbringing. I said the only attention I got in my life was when I was in the hospital at the age of seven after I jumped off a slide, expecting to fly. I attended a high school outside of my district, because the neighborhood where we lived became very rough. I admitted that I got beaten up quite often, as bullies would take advantage of me and kids my size. It got so bad that I had to pay protection fees just to be able to play in the playground after school. My dad would drive me to a school in a better neighborhood before he went to work in the morning and I would find public transportation to get me home. This lasted two years, until we moved to the area where the high school was located.

It was a very social school and you had to be in a club to avoid becoming a social outcast. The clubs seemed to control the school. These were good clubs with good kids who did a lot of work for local charities. We wore club jackets to and from school and during classes. The girls had their own social clubs and jackets. In fact, we would date many of the girls in our sister-clubs.

I saw the psychiatrist six times. His report to the court indicated I was working 70-80 hours per week at a non-lucrative and risky practice of providing divorce services for poor and lower middle-middle people. Prior to this episode, I had experienced years of sleep deprivation. I was never satisfied with myself, my performance or my life. The psychiatrist described my life has joyless. My daily routine consisted of rising around 4 a.m., working out at the gym and going to work. I'd get home around seven and be in bed no later than eight. On Sundays I would spend most of the day in bed. I was always dieting in an attempt to lose weight. My self-image was that of a short, over-weight, burned-out man who wasted 15 years of his life going the extra mile for unappreciative clients. I had no hobbies or interests outside of my work. I was chronically angry at my wife for how I felt she belittled me in front of our kids.

The psychiatrist said my health problems were significant. I was hypertensive for more than ten years. I had been treated with beta blockers which are known to cause a great deal of depression. I was a diabetic and took oral medication. I had to be careful with what I ate. I had been diagnosed with two herniated discs in my lumbar spine which caused me constant pain.

He spoke of my problematic anger problem and noted I was unable to express anger openly. I could be snide and sarcastic, but I rarely confronted conflict directly. I would withdraw and keep my anger to myself. He said I wasn't suicidal and showed no evidence of thought disorder. He said I was concerned for the welfare and livelihood of my family and those who worked for me.

The doctor stated that I was intelligent, earnest, and established good eye contact. He said that my affect is sober and depressive, but I can smile and be in good humor. My cognitive functions were intact and there was no evidence of delusional thinking. His impression was that I had been chronically depressed for many years, during which I suffered from sleep disturbances, overwork, and a tendency to overeat. His diagnosis was Anhedonia, which is the inability to gain pleasure from normally pleasurable experiences. Anhedonia is a core clinical feature of depression. He recommended that I take anti-depressant medications and requested that my general physician change my medications to help lessen the depression.

He described me as a complex man, raised in an emotionally deprived family. I had to suppress and repress many of my longings for dependency and affection. I never felt loved or accepted by my parents, experiences which are basic and necessary to the formation of healthy self-esteem. He said I felt inadequate and that nothing I had ever done was good enough. He claimed I felt I didn't deserve to be loved or to be happy and this sense of personal rejection caused me unreasonable and overwhelming feelings of worthlessness.

I had been incapable of seeking and getting gratification from dating, marriage and parenthood. Instead, I turned to my work for gratification. The psychiatrist said I left a successful career in personal-injury law, because it was emotionally ungratifying. He said I chose to represent the poor, because I could relate on a personal and emotional level with them, and therefore gratify my need for respect and appreciation. His report said I was very susceptible and vulnerable to the offer of comfort and affection from my client. She was grateful to me, but most important, she had traits which he said unconsciously represented my mother. He stated that I was a good candidate for psychotherapy and was willing to undergo it. Coupled with an appropriate change in my medication, he said it would greatly reduce or eliminate my susceptibility to advances from female clients. I learned a lot about myself from my psychiatric visits but as far as the Hearing Board was concerned, my doctor's testimony was nothing more than a perfunctory dog and pony show.

Chapter 13

FIGHTING BACK

As soon as the Hearing Board voted a Formal Complaint, the matter became very serious. Woodhouse and I needed to talk. We had to devise a plan for where we were going and what needed to be proved by our side. I felt I needed to fight back. I was seduced by her, rather than the other way around. She had concocted this story. That's what I thought should be the issue, that her credibility was shaky at best. Going through Afshan's file, I picked out factors that would show that everything I did for her legally was fully proper. Her statements against me were those of a vindictive woman who needed someone other than her husband to blame for all of her difficulties. As I sat in Woodhouse's office, I was thinking that my career was about to be destroyed. The system was set up so that a 'little guy' like my client could roar like a lion when questioned. By this I mean that a professional has no edge with his disciplinary watchdog group or Bar Association because the 'little guy' is given great power. I was getting madder and madder; it was time for me to defend myself.

Woodhouse appeared to be somewhat irritated that the matter had gone on this far. He told me he would request a meeting with the Inquiry Panel and ask for a reconsideration as to voting a Formal Complaint. He could tell by the tone of my voice that I was fed up with the whole situation. It was time for me to rock the boat, as it were.

I told him I had prepared an Order of Protection for my client, which meant that I honestly felt that she was being abused by her husband. I didn't question it. I obtained the divorce on her terms. I went the extra step of telling her that she should receive maintenance. When she refused, I advised her in writing that this was not the proper decision and was against my recommendations. She didn't follow my advice, just as she didn't follow the advice of her prior attorney when she settled that case without his knowledge. I never compromised her legal situation. I represented her zealously and diligently. The only money I ever gave her was for a cab ride home, which I did at her specific request. I never discounted my services, like someone who was receiving sexual favors for money might do. It was she who made the sexual advances. She never discharged me and never asked for her money back. She never complained about her legal services. She received an itemized bill each month and never complained about that either.

When I gave my statement to the DDC, I had no knowledge that she had already given a statement. Since I didn't have the opportunity to look at her statement before I gave mine, my credibility couldn't be tainted. She, on the other hand, said things which could easily be disproved. For instance, she said I asked my associate not to work on her case. That couldn't be true because my associate took her to court each and every time. I never went to court with her, except for the time when her divorce became final. She said I was always handling her case, even though my associate handled it throughout the litigation. There was also a second associate who was involved in her case on several occasions.

My associates and I did professional and competent work for her. This wasn't her first divorce and it was apparent, to me at least, that all she wanted to do was punish her husband and her attorney. And the DDC attorney was happy to contribute to the latter. Afshan never talked of intercourse or making love until the DDC attorney brought the subjects up. "Yes, he wanted to do it," she said. "He wanted to make love." Seems to me, if that had really happened, she would have brought it up on her own. Then she was asked if I ever used the word "fuck" and she said yes.

The truth was that I never violated any of the statues. Even if I had done something sexual with her, there are no laws against having a consensual relationship between a client and a professional. Of course, there could be a conflict from that behavior, but it would have to be proved like everything else. As far as my representation of her, it had no effect on the outcome of her case. She had filed a complaint with the DDC because I told her she was legally obligated to give her husband visitation rights for the children. Since she never asked for "supervised visitation" with her children, her husband probably wasn't abusive to her like she said he was. If he was abusive, why wouldn't she ask for supervised visitation? If she gave him those rights, it would have been an admission on her part that he had won. She was not about to let that happen.

Surely the DDC must have understood that I deal with a very abusive type of clientele. Usually the women have been scorned, abused, ridiculed and tossed around like a rag doll by their husbands. This is what a divorce lawyer has to deal with every day of the week. We need to practice psychology in addition to practicing law, just so we can complete the business at hand. We have to understand the situation and allow the client to vent. You're dealing more with their emotions than you are with logic. After awhile, you forget how mentally exhausting the days are. To say it's an occupational hazard is an understatement. Somehow, I had managed to stay afloat.

I was so infuriated with this case that I actually started to respect myself again. Talk about unintended consequences. The more Woodhouse and I talked, the more aggressive I became. I felt I had been taken advantage of and I blew off a lot of steam. We talked the issue to death. The bottom line was that Woodhouse was going to ask the Inquiry Panel for Reconsideration. And then we'd see what happened.

Chapter 14

THE PANEL

As we sat in the Reception Room at the DDC's office, Woodhouse whispered to me that I should just be truthful when answering their questions. He reminded me that all of my answers should be the same as the ones I gave in my Sworn Statement. He said I'd have to bite my tongue and not have any outbursts of anger. I knew I had to remain silent no matter what my client said. I also knew this would be an uphill battle.

The hearing room was large with 12-foot ceilings. The three panel members sat behind a long table in high back chairs is if they were on the Supreme Court. An American flag was draped on one side and the County flag was draped on the other. The Panel didn't wear robes - they weren't members of the judiciary - but the feeling I got was this was a very, very important hearing. There seemed to be an extreme amount of tension in the room and I was very nervous. Woodhouse had done his homework and brought 20-30 pages of notes to back up his opening statement. If this didn't turn out to be a Kangaroo Court, I figured I had a pretty good chance to prevail.

After Afshan and I were sworn in, Woodhouse approached the podium. He placed his notes and glasses on the podium and began to address the Panel. He said he was there on my behalf and felt strongly that the Panel should reconsider their voting of a Formal Complaint. He indicated that a psychiatric report was issued and that the entire matter was a "close call." During my 15-year career in divorce law, approximately six times a month I dealt with women who said they were beaten by their husband.

He emphasized that no one other than this woman had ever accused me of any sexual conduct with them. He explained that I had fought off the advances of seductive, emotionally upset women for years, and further stated that I had resisted Afshan, too. He said all of the things Afshan had included in her statement were absolutely false.

Woodhouse claimed that my law firm was one of the best in terms of our reputation for truth and veracity among the Judges. He described the type of clients that we represented as abusive people who had no problem abusing their own attorney. Though it was very difficult to deal with these clients, he emphasized that my firm did very good legal and professional work for everyone we represented.

He admitted from time to time I would see Afshan in my office at 5:00 or 5:30 p.m., but that I saw many clients after 5:00 p.m., as most lawyers do. Though my client said I set these appointments at a time when we could be alone, we usually had lawyers in our office as late as 8:00 p.m. That meant the chances of the two of us being alone in the office were almost nil. Woodhouse acknowledged that my first response to the allegations of sexual misconduct was a denial and that I recanted or qualified my denial soon after giving it. My new denial showed she had attempted to seduce me but had not succeeded, and that I had resisted all of her attempts. He said there was no conflict of interest and no indication that either I or my firm would withdraw from her case or would have handled it any differently than the way we ultimately did.

Woodhouse described my client as a bitter, out-of-control woman who would constantly demean me. She would come in unexpectedly and make scenes at the office when I said I couldn't see her. He explained this behavior is familiar to divorce lawyers, because clients are transferring their guilt from their spouse to their attorney. He emphasized over and over that she was highly seductive every time she came to our offices.

Woodhouse went on to say that I took pride in the work I did. He considered me to be an asset to the legal profession, because most lawyers don't want to work in the low-income arena. He claimed I was one of the very few attorneys who answers his calls at night through the answering service, and that I carried a pager 24/7. He was painting me as a committed and conscientious attorney, rather than the devious, sexual predator that the DDC wanted everybody to believe I was. Listening to Woodhouse was one of the most satisfying experiences of my adult life.

Woodhouse claimed that what Afshan said happened had never happened before in my career. He said I had tried in every possible way to demonstrate my good faith and reminded the panel that there was no law against what might have taken place between me and my client. Even if there were, I did not succumb to her sexual advances. He suggested that the Supreme Court should have a rule that makes any single sexual conduct between a lawyer and a client a conflict of interest, but that no such rule existed today. Nor is there any clear-cut rule on what constitutes sexual contact.

If this matter went to a Complaint, Woodhouse said most of the damage would already have been done and I would lose, and lose big, whether or not I ended up winning the case. He believed the filing of a Formal Complaint would destroy my marriage and my good name. He said I didn't harm the client in any legal way and that her case was handled as properly as it could have been handled. He pointed out the big discrepancies in the client's description of what happened between her and I. He also said they couldn't possibly rule against me when there is no rule of law to go to for guidance in this matter. If the Panel talked to every one of my female clients, they would find that none of them had a similar experience to tell. This was the only time I had ever been accused of such behavior and that didn't reflect well on my accuser.

The Prosecutor now had the opportunity to ask me questions in front of the Panel. The panel seemed focussed on assessing the potential for how this episode might negatively impact the client. I told them I recognized the potential for harm to a client. I mentioned the name of her previous lawyer and that he had nothing good to say about her when I spoke to him. The Prosecutor wasn't looking for that and told me so.

It was a very solemn hearing. There was no humor, no side conversations or the like. Woodhouse and I left as soon as the Panel adjourned. I complimented him on his fine opening speech and felt he was very much on my side. He thought the accusations against me were highly questionable. To suspend a professional's license or to destroy his career and his family certainly was a case of overkill, given the lack of credible evidence to support my accuser's contentions. The matter, we both thought, should have been ended at this stage. Shoulda, coulda, woulda.

Chapter 15

THE PRESS

My attorney called me with the bad news. The Inquiry Panel had voted to deny our Motion to Reconsider the issuance of a Formal Complaint. The Prosecutor had orchestrated a case against me under the theory that I was a threat to society and should not be allowed to continue practicing law. Did the Prosecutor have a personal vendetta? Was this case merely a stepping stone to put her on the fast track for career advancement and fame? It would ultimately have been the first case that would be decided by the Supreme Court of our state as to whether sexual contact of any kind between an attorney and a client is illegal or unethical, even it's consensual. But, in this case I denied her accusations.

The Prosecutor had written a letter to my client right after the hearing and reminded her that the "press" was going to be at her doorstep and she should not talk to reporters. Woodhouse said the case might be reported to the press by the Prosecutor and said it would be in my best interests if I could prevent this from going to the media. He agreed that a Motion to bar my name from the proceedings would be desirable and I got his permission to prepare and file the motion by myself. Time was of the essence here.

I had a contact at the Supreme Court office that day, a clerk who would rush the Motion into the Emergency Supreme Court Judge that was sitting. For one of the few times in my career, I wasn't ready when my contact was in a position to receive the Motion. The influence I thought I had was not there on this particular day, nor was any semblance of personal good luck. My Emergency Motion to bar my name was denied by a Supreme Court Justice and I knew the consequences from that were going to be severe.

What do you do when depression takes over your mind and body? You don't know which way to turn or which way to go. My family had no knowledge of what was going on. I had been pretty good at keeping everything from my wife, my children and my office personnel. That was about to change. I could see it all clearly now. My wife would approach me, crying hysterically, and raving what I maniac I was. I could see my kids being unwilling to even hear my side of the story. I could picture myself packing my bags and leaving the house with my tail tucked between my legs. I didn't know where I would go because any place I went would have to be devoid of people. Yes, I considered suicide.

No one wants to be publically humiliated in the news, because you know it will probably destroy your career, your family, and every dream and aspiration that you ever had. If I looked people in the eye, they'd be so embarrassed for me that they'd turn away in silence. All they would see is that big scarlet letter painted all over me. The scales that balance life versus death were out of balance. That's what happens when depression takes over your mind and body? You spiral almost totally out of control. Thank God for the almost.

Like I said before, this case should have been dropped. However, that wasn't the agenda of the Prosecutor. She was a young woman in the early stages of her career. She hadn't made a name for herself, wasn't married, had never practiced law and had no idea of the pressures, problems and abuse that a lawyer endures in my kind of practice. She had no clue as to what "real life" was all about. Yet, with a flick of her finger, she could wash away an entire person's career and destroy his family life.

I started making a mental list of who I was going to call. Obviously, my wife would be first, the children would be second, then my closest relatives and my office personnel. My staff would we very worried and I wondered if any of them would immediately quit. The publicity was going to be very, very bad and certainly would not help their image in the Courthouse. The key for me, of course, was how my wife would react.

Chapter 16

FENDING FOR MYSELF

I was born in New York during World War II and eventually became the middle child of three children. I was like the spoke of the wheel that didn't fit, the proverbial square peg in the round hole. Neither of my parents were strong personalities. As a result, nobody in my family really ever influenced me. They basically paid no attention to me. My parents never asked any questions and I received absolutely no guidance. I never felt loved at all. To my mother, I didn't exist. My dad never took me to a ballgame or anywhere else for that matter. He didn't take my brother and sister anywhere, either. The only warmth I got from my father was when he taught me how to drive. He only did so because I threw a fit.

My father always did whatever my mother told him to do. He wore an apron and often cleaned the house. Mom was a college graduate, but she never worked a day in her life. My mother was a spoiled woman and it showed by the way she brought up her children. She never prepared a meal for us. The three of us were latchkey kids and I learned to fend for myself at a fairly early age. Mom was a social butterfly and her activities outside of her home occupied all of her time. Her friends were more important to her than we were. My older brother and I thought she was a bitch. After my father died, my mother put an ad in the Sentinel for a husband who liked working around the house.

I flunked the Bar Exam the first time I took it. The night before my second attempt, I was studying when my mother called me from Manhattan. She had forgotten some trophies she was supposed to give out at an event and demanded that I bring them to her. I said no and she threatened to throw me out of the house. I was desperately worried about my career possibilities, but my mother wanted me to stop studying and bring her some trophies the night before a bar exam.

My Grandfather on my mother's side came from Poland where he built ships. He met my grandmother somewhere outside of Poland. I don't know if there was ever any evidence that they'd been married but everybody assumed they were. My grandfather was the first plumber in the city of New York, and started the city's first plumbing supply shop. He also branched into making large canisters to fit over gas pipes so they could hang the new electric fixtures that Thomas Edison had invented.

I was four years younger than my older brother and seven years older than my younger sister. My mother was nine months pregnant on my 7th birthday. Sure enough, her water broke at my party and they rushed her to the hospital to give birth. It was bad enough that I already had to share my birthday with a national holiday, New Year's Day. Now I had to share it with my sister, too. I found out years later that I had blocked out memories of living with my younger sister for many years, because she somehow participated in the breaking up of that birthday party when I was seven years old.

For the remainder of her life, I would call her on the morning of January 1st to wish her a happy birthday. We never celebrated our birthdays together, but I could never forget my birthday was my sister's birthday, too. I was babysitting her one night when I was 11 or 12 years old and she was jumping on her bed and landed on the window sill. She split her nose open and bled profusely. I don't remember if they took her to a hospital, if I got a hold of my mother and father, or if an ambulance came. According to a psychiatrist that I saw many years later, the reason that I blocked her out of my psyche was either because of the birthday party or because my sister got injured on my watch. In any case, I have no other memory of her living in the same house with us when we were kids.

When I was attending my first grammar school, I would walk a mile and a half to school by myself. On one occasion I gathered all of my friends around a slide in the schoolyard during recess. I climbed to the top and told everybody I was going to be Superman. I've been told that I dived head first off the slide and landed on a concrete slab. They took me to a local hospital, but a room wasn't available. Instead, they cordoned off an aisle in a hallway, placed temporary curtains, brought in a bed and hospitalized me with a very severe head concussion. I stayed there for two weeks. The aisle was my home for two weeks. For the next two or three years, I couldn't look at light and I needed to be kept in a dark room. I had chronic headaches during that entire period. Ironically, I've rarely had a headache since then.

I was the captain of the patrol boys, captain of the hall monitors, captain of the movie projector people. I got those jobs because I wanted them more than any of the other kids did - all three of them. We were the first grammar school in the city of New York to publish its own newspaper and I was the editor. I made my rounds checking all the street corners and making sure all the patrol boys were on duty. Because I was short there were instances where kids would bully me. I was a very fast runner and after they bullied me, I would punch them in the mouth and run away. I think I did that two or three times and it was a very rewarding experience. There was a major element of danger to it but I loved it.

During my high school years, my brother and I would stand on the streets of Harlem where we sold the first African American dolls in the city of New York. I sold them while he was making deals with the politicians on the street and ordering goods. We stored all the goods in our grandfather's plumbing supply store and we'd pick them up on a Sunday morning. We had hundreds of toys and we'd sell them on cold winter days. We also sold beer and pop at Yankee Stadium, the Polo Grounds, Madison Square Garden and all the other sporting venues. I sold the beer before I was 21 because I lied about my age. If I were selling ice cream I'd give my brother half of my ice cream and if he was selling Cokes he'd give me half of them and then we both had a variety of items to sell. Because of that, we were able to empty our trays faster than most other vendors. We didn't want to get robbed at the end of the day on our way out, so we'd put the cash in a big envelope and mail it to ourselves from a mailbox in the basement of the stadium.

I followed my brother to college and pledged his fraternity. There was a lot of dating going on because it was mandatory that pledges had to date so many girls in a specified period of time. I had ADHD and I was usually behind in my grades and would take women to a library on a study date. Apart from being forced to do it, I have to admit it was a pretty good idea.

In those days fraternity houses didn't have house mothers. That meant we had to take even more crap from the fraternity brothers. Pledges had to wear three dead fish around their waists for two weeks and weren't allowed to shower or clean up during that 14-day period. I smelled so bad that the Class Proctor would meet me at the door and tell me to sit in the back of the room. Sometimes he wouldn't even allow me in the room.

Hell Week was just that. They once put me into my leather jacket and hung me on a hanger in the closet. They tarred and feathered us each night. We had to eat candied ants and raw eggs, which they would drop into our mouths from the third story balcony. We had to keep a goldfish alive in the toilet so when we took a dump we had to take the goldfish out, put it in a container to keep it alive, and sit there holding it as we relieved ourselves.

We learned how to dish things out ourselves. We did such terrible things that it's uncomfortable just thinking about it. Guys in my pledge class greased the fire escape with oil, then threw a smoke bomb in the dorm and locked the doors so people couldn't get out. Members had to go down the fire escape where, very fortunately, nobody killed themselves. While certain members were sleeping, we would tie a piece of string around their penis and attach it to the top of the bed. When they got out of the bed, they would have their penis attached to the bed. We would put water balloons in between the springs of the mattress above them. When the guy got in the bed above them, the water balloon would burst and splatter all over the member on the bottom. We weren't bad kids, just survivors. Plus, the things that we did earned us the respect of the members. Turns out, they were just as insecure as we were.

Chapter 17

OUT IN THE OPEN

It was about 5:30 p.m. when I got back to my office to start making the calls. Thinking that the story might make the Six O'Clock News, I decided that I would call my wife on the phone instead of waiting to talk to her in person. There was no time for that now. The chances of her being blindsided by the news were very great. I closed my door and went to my desk. My hand quivered slightly and my heart was pounding. When I dialed my house, I was hoping that my wife wouldn't be home. Maybe I had overreacted and the story wasn't going to make the news. However, she answered the phone and I engaged in some small talk until I dropped the bomb.

"Honey, we have a problem," I said. I told her that a client had accused me of some sexual impropriety, but that they were all false. I told her a Formal Complaint had been filed against me. I again categorically denied all of the allegations, but told her I had to defend myself and it might go public as early as this evening. She immediately reacted by saying, "We'll get through this together." I'm sure she detected a hint of tears from my end. I asked her to give me the phone number of our closest relatives and she did. I told her I intended to call each of them as fast as I could to diminish the impact of them seeing my story on the news.

I was surprised when I heard her voice perk up. She told me what we were having for supper in an apparent attempt to calm me down. I told her I loved her and always would. She replied in the same fashion, but I knew she felt hurt, scorned and abused by me at that moment. The next person I called was my sister-in-law and told her I wasn't guilty of anything. "I'm sure you did nothing wrong," she said, "and I appreciate your letting me know." It was a very short conversation. I called my other relatives quickly, one by one. Some I reached and some I didn't. Some asked me inappropriate questions and I responded as best I could. The bottom line was that I denied everything. I hadn't talked to some of these relatives in years, but I didn't want anybody reading more into my situation than there really was. I felt my character was being assassinated.

There wasn't an ounce of energy left in me when I walked through our front door. When I saw my wife, I put my arms around her and cried like a baby. I went into a low-key tirade about how some fucking people have no qualms about destroying one's career to further their own ambitions. We hugged for a while and I then I changed my clothes. I went into a more detailed explanation as to what took place and how I denied it all. I asked her if she saw the news and she said she had. "The anchorman reported that a lawyer was charged with sexually molesting a client and they had your photo on the screen," she said. She joked that it wasn't my best picture.

Then I lost it. I demanded she tell me every specific thing that was said and how it was said. It was as if I had put her on the stand and was cross-examining her. I knew how grossly unfair I was being but I couldn't help it. I was close to being out of control with the one person with whom I should have never been out of control. The television report sounded bad. My God, I didn't molest anybody! I was depressed, tired, exhausted and I had enough of this entire day. I became somewhat calm and made sure that she was calm enough to handle the problem. She clearly understood the predicament I was in and agreed that she would handle the situation the best she could. I hated to put her in this position but I needed her help right now. I needed her to have at least some confidence in me, too, because I didn't want to break up our family. I needed to tell the children. I knew I might be short with them, because I was thoroughly exhausted. Donna agreed to call them and talk to them.

I went to bed but didn't sleep a wink. I woke up as irritable as I was the night before. My head hung low as I got into my car for the drive to work. I knew this was going to be another day of hell. I had appointments with clients that I couldn't cancel. Plus, I still had to tell my staff what had taken place and I needed to follow up with my children.

As soon as everybody arrived, I called an office meeting in the library. It appeared that some of the people knew what was going on, but none of them would admit it. There were 15 of us who sat in the large conference room. Everyone was anxious to find out why they were there because their days had already begun. Some were nervous because they had to be in court in 30 minutes and still had to prepare their files. Others had clients that were coming in soon and they needed to prepare for them also. Mornings, particularly Monday mornings, are always tense and unpleasant. This is the time we sometimes refer to as the calm before the storm. If we have one calm day out of five, we're appreciative of our good fortune. So, this was a meeting nobody really wanted to be at.

I told everybody I'd have them out of there in 10 minutes. I explained that the DDC had been investigating a complaint filed by one of my clients that I had sexual contact with her. I denied all the allegations and told them the Panel had voted a Formal Complaint. I reassured them that their jobs were not in jeopardy and that this was a matter that would be easily overcome at the Supreme Court level, if not sooner. My staff knew the abuse that we take, each and every day. They didn't put much credence in the allegations because they knew that the next client who walked through our doors might very well end up being their own personal client from hell. I asked if any of them had seen the news clip last night and it was apparent that none of them had seen it. Well, thank God for that!

After my staff meeting, I called my kids to follow-up on what their mother had told them. I presented my story in the best light that I could. They sounded satisfied, but I got the feeling that they were still trying to process everything that had taken place.

The Daily Herald arrived at my office and I saw the front page headline. "Lawyer Charged in Sex Scandal" seemed to jump off the page. There was an entire article on me and the allegations I faced. I was devastated. Still, I showed it to everybody in the office and told them this is what we were up against and that I needed their support. I was the main subject of the morning's news and I realized that the regular newspapers were going to be just as devastating. I immediately went down to the newspaper vendor in the lobby of my building and bought every newspaper he had and brought them up to my office. I wanted to return unseen but my receptionist saw me. She obviously reported this to everybody else in the office because the tension that morning was palpable. It felt like so much air had been sucked out of the room that there wasn't enough to go around. My breathing was so shallow it's a wonder I didn't pass out. I think the only reason I didn't was because every so often I'd inhale deeply. One good, deep breath every ten minutes or so was what passed for respiration to me.

I went through each newspaper until I found the article about myself. As I read it, I got more furious, depressed, agitated and stunned. By God, where did they get all this information? How did they get a copy of my client's Sworn Statement? The day had barely started and I had to try to get back to some semblance of normalcy. Otherwise. I was going to go down for the count.

My meeting with my office staff went reasonably well. I knew they'd be approached by lawyers as they walked through the halls and corridors of the Courthouse. I didn't address every possible contingency and I'm sure they had a lot of questions that I didn't have time to answer. Things like, what are they to say, how are they to react? There's only so much information you can impart to people in a 10-minute meeting. Furthermore, this meeting was not something I had planned or even thought about until this situation came along.

I called a well-known news anchor friend of mine and asked him if I should hold a press conference. He immediately faxed over a one page "instruction" sheet which he titled, "Preparation." He said I should have copies of my statement ready for distribution, if I decided to make one. He said I should be prepared to read my statement over the phone if asked by a reporter or a news producer. Other than that, he told me I shouldn't make any comments about the case. Under no circumstances should I agree to do a television interview. If pressed by a reporter, I should politely explain that cases should be tried in Court, rather than in the media. I knew very well that in explosive cases such as mine, reporters don't let the facts get in the way of a good story.

If I held a press conference, I would touch on the following points. The charges in the Complaint were not true. Evidence would clearly show my innocence and I'd be vindicated. I would vigorously defend my reputation against untrue statements and offer my spotless 25-year record of representing clients as a defense against my client's charges. It occurred to me that if I had a press conference, they would question me on every sexual detail they could find. The media would just as soon try an entire case in the media where they could drive the conversation. Answering "no comment" over and over would make me look guilty. First and foremost, I had my family and friends to consider. They had already suffered at my hand and a press conference would only make things worse for me, and them. Once the press gets even a little taste of the blood in the water, they turn into the equivalent of man-eating sharks.

I decided not to make a bad situation worse. Why give the press another chance to attack and discredit me? I had already shocked and embarrassed my family and friends, bringing disharmony to my relationship with every one of them. Would a second "jolt" generated by a press release or press conference make things better or worse in this regard? Looking at the situation as objectively as I could convinced me to stand pat. I wasn't so naive to think that the whole problem was going to go away, no matter what I did. But doing nothing was at least something I could control. Creating another self-inflicted wound for myself would be like pouring gasoline on a fire that I was trying to put out. Thank God for logic.

Chapter 18

DIVORCE LAWYERS - A RARE BREED

I was apprehensive and extremely hypersensitive on the day of my appointment with Dr. Geisler. I tried to calm down by telling myself all I had to do was sit there and tell him the truth. His office was in the Department of Psychiatry at St. Mary's Hospital.

There wasn't a couch in Dr. Geisler's office. Every psychiatrist is supposed to have a couch, right? He was in his 60's, with grey hair, a small grey goatee and a moustache. Other than that, the most prominent thing about him was his belly which hung over the waistband of his trousers. The doctor was sitting at his desk, no more than four feet away from me. His desk faced a wall and he had to swivel around in order to make eye contact with me. I found this annoying and our positioning made it seem to me like I was the shrink and he was on the hot seat.

We made small talk and he said he always wanted to be a lawyer. We both felt that most lawyers are frustrated doctors and that most doctors are frustrated lawyers. The law fascinated him and that's why murder mysteries were his favorite books. He asked me why I was there and I told him what had taken place thus far. I told him I would get psychiatric help if he thought I needed it. I told him if it hadn't been for the prosecutor's wanting to make a name for herself, I wouldn't be here.

He wanted to know about my childhood. I've read several articles which claim that being a middle child often carries difficulties. The middle child is generally the neglected one who has to fend for himself and be independent at an early age. The middle child is usually the nicest of the three, in part because he has to "survive" without the aid of the parents. I told Dr. Geisler that being short brought additional consequences for me and had a significant impact on my early teens. I don't remember having any anger management problems back then, though they did blossom later in my life. The Napoleon complex manifested itself only after I got out of college. Dr. Geisler asked me about my medical history. I told him of my high blood pressure, my back problems, my diabetes and the various medications I took. He particularly wanted to know how long I had been treated for diabetes.

Our second session took place three days later. Divorce lawyers are able to obtain relevant information from their clients very quickly. For instance, I never needed 20 sessions with a client to find out if one of the spouses had a playmate on the side. Psychiatrists, on the other hand, seem to take forever to come to their conclusions. They sometimes go five or six sessions before even asking that particular question. The fact is, they rarely ask questions. They allow you to formulate your own thoughts so you can say to yourself, "Oh, my God, this is what's really going on!"

Most divorce lawyers think we practice psychiatry without a license and that we're damn good at it. In a high volume legal practice, you have to put your head into that of your clients. That's how you find out what makes them tick; what kind of emotions they display; what their feelings are toward their spouse, their children and their parents. You need to do this rapidly because you usually have less than an hour with them. You ask direct questions because you're looking for immediate, unambiguous responses.

I don't think Dr. Geisler considered me to be a model patient. I'd preface my comments by saying things like, "Do you really want to hear this?" I always felt I was boring him. I know that many of my clients actually bored me with unnecessary details, so I felt it was my obligation to keep Geisler awake. Venting can be incredibly boring to a professional who hears these kinds of ravings day after day. So, I regaled him with stories from my college days and I enjoyed telling him what took place.

My final two sessions with Dr. Geisler were quite interesting. I told him the legal work I did before starting my own divorce practice. I initially worked as a Claims Adjuster for an insurance company on a part-time basis while going through law school. I learned what injuries were worth in dollars and became very good at analyzing personal injury cases. After passing the State Bar exam, I worked for the law firm that represented the same insurance company that employed me. I soon became head of the firm's Subrogation Department and defended insureds in lawsuits.

A year later I went to a second firm where I became a good trial lawyer, primarily because of how much time I spent in court. Two years later I went to a firm that dealt with a high volume of personal injury cases. I was one of three trial lawyers there and I handled myself very well. I was ranked number seven in the County in jury verdicts one year. In a city of more than 40,000 attorneys, relatively few were trial lawyers. The public probably doesn't realize that most lawyers never appear in Court.

I would go from one Courtroom to the next and had very little time for home life or relaxation during those years. It made me start to reconsider my goals and I had to admit to myself that I didn't find the work very gratifying. The few chances I had to talk to clients were always about their injuries and never about real life. I missed the banter between me and my clients. That made me switch to Family Law where I had an opportunity to play a significant and helpful role in their lives.

There are many aspects of handling a divorce that involve making changes that will help your client, his or her family, their children and their relationships to others. We're placed in a situation where we have to make decisions on behalf of our clients that we feel will be of some benefit to them. Lower and middle income divorce clients, whether they be paternity clients or people with visitation or child support problems, all tend to be the same. Most of them live day to day, without a safety net to rely on. It's difficult for them to hire a professional like a doctor or a lawyer, and be able to pay them on a regular basis. As a result, I often ended up receiving 25 or 50 cents on the dollar in a great many cases. I chose this clientele because it was easier to quickly build up a practice with poor people that it was with wealthy ones. Wealthy clients expect to visit spacious and beautifully furnished offices. If you don't have the money to create that kind of office, you're basically forced to go with middle or lower income clients.

In the Family Divorce arena, the poor and middle class are extremely abusive towards their attorneys. By abusive, I mean they would call at all hours of the night demanding responses and actions to deal with their problems. They never begin a conversation by saying, "I apologize for calling you so late." If you're waiting for that kind of consideration, don't hold your breath. Clients think because they pay you, they own you. People whose lives have been essentially devoid of power, love to pretend that they now have some. It's a variation of the bully mentality except most of my clients have always been on the wrong end of those encounters.

Chapter 19

STARTING ALL OVER AGAIN

I learned five major lessons during my law career. First, you need money to get justice. Second, everything is political in the court system. Third, women are taking over the legal system and a majority of them resent male attorneys. If you attempt to tell them the law, they hang up on you as though you were their spouse. Fourth, lawyers are still regarded as the equal of car salesmen. Advertising is the only way we can bring up our images. Ads are very powerful. Lastly, once a lawyer becomes a judge, their personality changes and their attitude towards you as a friend is gone.

There are things I would change about the legal system. Frankly, I'd revamp a lot of it. Being in court is a complete waste of time. You often wait around for hours and then the judge will set a new date a month out. You can't question the judge. We're at his mercy. If he's horny, attorneys suffer. If he forgot to buy his playmate a birthday present, and you're in court when he realizes it, you suffer. One hundred cases come before a judge in a day. It takes two or three hours to start a trial, and 30 or 40 hours to finish each one. It's easy to see the numbers don't add up. Nobody's happy and everybody's pissed. It's like trying to grow justice in a petri dish. After a few thousand experiments, the legal system might theoretically figure things out.

In federal court, you don't have to file documents. You only have to send them to the opposing counsel. If there is a certain scenario, then a certain law will apply. They could do that with maintenance now, and a lot of laws could be passed eliminating the need to sit in court and draft various documents. Right now, courts have petitions for everything. They've inadvertently given individuals the ability to gum up the works, and to do it legally. Why not just stand in front of a judge and say the husband is not paying child support? Why make us submit all the paperwork? It's a gross waste of time, money and resources, but bringing attention to the problem is something most attorneys simply don't have the guts to do.

I'm a very organized person and methodical in the way I do things. I have a system for everything and display a lot of ingenuity. I've probably created more office forms for lawyers to use than any other attorney has. Many hundreds of lawyers have copied my contracts, without my permission, and not given me any royalties.

There have been some insignificant legal changes over the years. The word "divorce" was changed to "Dissolution of Marriage" because it had a negative psychological effect on men. We changed the word "custody" to "parenting time". We changed all the words, because we didn't want anybody to be offended. And we didn't want to offend the church. So we eliminated 12 of 13 grounds for divorce. The church wouldn't allow all grounds to be eliminated, but there is a law now being formulated in Albany to eliminate all grounds for divorce. We never used cheating on a spouse as grounds for divorce because it was too hard to prove. So we used mental cruelty, which occurs when one spouse yelled and the other spouse got a headache.

All pleadings start out with an archaic paragraph, followed by a litany of paragraphs which are supposed to inform the judge why you're there. I noticed none of the judges ever read the whereas clause at the end of the document. It made no sense to me for it to be at the end, so I put it at the front. I always would interrupt long rambles by my clients and tell them I'm only interested in the bottom line. It's called cutting to the chase, an extremely useful tactic when you're pressed for time and inundated with work. When I tried to do it in court, I was criticized for it. The Judge was Jewish and I expected him to start singing Tradition from Fiddler On The Roof.

———————

All parties to litigation have the right by law to attend the deposition of a witness. Dr. Geisler was set to give his deposition at 2 p.m. at the DDC's offices and his deposition could make or break me. The Complaint filed by the client had festered into an uncontrollable situation with criminal charges and disbarment becoming an increasing possibility.

Worried, I decided to switch lawyers for the third time because I didn't think Woodhouse had accomplished anything favorable to this point. It was very distasteful to me to have to start all over again with a new attorney. I went to see a former Assistant Prosecutor for the United States Justice Department. He was the "heavyweight" I felt I needed. His name was Jeff Stone and he had recently left the Office of the Attorney General. In less than two years he had established a thriving legal practice with 25 attorneys working under him. Most of their criminal litigation was white collar crime, and several were politicians who had done something stupid that put their entire careers at risk. After speaking with him over the phone, I scheduled an appointment. I knew this was going to be very expensive and I did not relish having to borrow money from my family or friends.

Stone's reception room was lavish. Next to the couch where I sat was a large modern sculpture. Three more end tables in the large reception area each had smaller sculptures. There were three large, expensive-looking paintings on the walls, and they blended well with the beige, checkered patterns of the wallpaper. All the while, thoughts were going through my head as rapidly as gunfire. This is no way to live, I thought to myself.

I was escorted to Stone's office, where he got up from his chair and greeted me with a firm handshake. He was 5' 10" tall, fairly trim and I guessed him to be in his early fifties. The first thing I noticed about Stone was the beautiful US Flag cuff links he wore. Obviously, the Attorney General's Office decorum was still ingrained in his dress and mannerisms. He greeted me with the type of warmth and professionalism that I needed at this point. His office was so luxurious that it reminded me of the suite of rooms that are given to high rollers in Las Vegas. He had two leather couches with three matching chairs, a cocktail table, and a little area where he could sit and talk with his clients instead of having them feel intimidated by sitting in front of his desk. I wrote him a $5,000 check because I felt comfortable enough with him to retain his firm.

Stone said the first thing he wanted to do was talk to Dr. Geisler at his office and go over his notes. That was reassuring and I knew in my heart that choosing him was the right decision. Even if things went south, I knew I'd be able to look back and tell myself that I tried my very best by hiring the best people. We parted after two hours and I told him I'd send over a letter authorizing him to take over for Woodhouse. The form is called a Substitution of Attorneys. It was an unpleasant thing to do, but I knew it couldn't be avoided.

Stone and I talked for 45 minutes before walking over to the DDC's office for Dr. Geisler's deposition. Stone found Geisler's notes to be somewhat disorganized and he thought it might present a problem when he testified. Some doctors will dictate their notes immediately after a session and have them typewritten in the patient's chart. Others, like Dr. Geisler, can't keep up with the patient's words and the notes become somewhat unreadable. Still, Stone felt that Geisler's history and qualifications would make a very good impression with the DDC. It was his opinion that the deposition would come out in my favor but, as we all know, there's no such thing as a sure thing.

Stone went into chambers to have preliminary discussions regarding the ground rules. As I sat in the Courtroom, Dr. Geisler arrived and I introduced him to the Court Reporter. He asked me how long this would take and I estimated two or three hours. I think he thought he would be out of there in 15 to 30 minutes. I didn't talk to him about his testimony, because that was my attorney's job. The DDC's attorney looked as though she was ready to go. She gave my attorney a great deal of respect, because everyone in Manhattan knew and respected him. She addressed him as Mr. Stone. It was a small point in my favor.

Dr. Geisler was asked about his qualifications. He was President of the State Psychiatric Society for many years, a member of various Ethics Committees, the New York Psychoanalytic Society, the American Psychiatric Association, and others. They asked him about testifying in criminal cases and every time I heard the word criminal it felt like I was being hit in the head with a hammer.

Dr. Geisler said he had no knowledge of my case until I gave him copies of some newspaper articles. He based all of his opinions on my discussions with him. The DDC quickly asked what he thought about my present condition. He said I suffered from dysthymia, which he explained was a moderately severe form of depression. In his opinion, I was eminently treatable and he said he'd made considerable progress with psychotherapy and the use of antidepressants. He said he had prescribed Prozac for me. He believed I showed an unconscious sense of guilt that I carried from childhood. He said I had dysthymia, a mood disorder with the same physical and cognitive problems as depression, but with less severe but longer-lasting symptoms. He said the condition worsens over a lifetime. If untreated, it would continue to worsen but he thought his treatment of me would resolve those problems and alleviate my depression.

At this point, Dr. Geisler admitted he was having difficulty reading his own handwriting. They asked him to read his notes exactly as they were and not to add anything that he independently recalled. He detailed each of the appointments I had with my client. He characterized me as a workaholic who doesn't go on vacations. He claimed this drove me crazy and had notes that indicated I couldn't stand myself.

He felt my constantly calling the answering service at night was a compulsive act. The fact that I would answer my pager 24/7 was to him an example of compulsive behavior. He claimed my Attention Deficit Hyperactive Disorder (ADHD) made everything I did all the more difficult. The doctor described me as harassed and harried and that I seemed to always be very tense and depressed. He thought I was extremely frightened and said I sighed as I talked, eyes glazed and sometimes dropping. He was amazed that I received a telephone call during the first session, because all of his patients who carried cell phones would turn them off during his sessions. He had no idea why I was so scared and depressed. He asked me to have my blood tested, which was something he asked of all his patients.

He said I appeared to be upset and fit to be tied during our second session, because a flood in the basement of my office building had destroyed hundreds of my client files. He found me overwhelmed by it and that I clearly overreacted to the situation. Throughout all of our sessions, he said I would overreact whenever there was a problematic situation occurring in my life.

Dr. Geisler spent a great deal of time talking about the kinds of clients I served. He said I knew they felt bad about themselves; I could relate to them because I also felt bad about myself. Poor clients would open up to me quickly because I treated them with compassion. He claimed I felt good about working for them, because it was like I was working for myself. "The guy who is this ignorant person, who is socially inept, who is his client, he sees as if he were helping himself, because the client is him," said Geisler. He claimed I overly identify with my clients and I live through every one of their traumas. He said it meant I put myself at risk for hypertension and depression, because I couldn't distance myself from what my client did. I have to admit that I was surprised to hear his diagnosis. At times I felt like I was watching a documentary of myself.

He was asked why I would put myself at risk over and over again. He surmised it was because of the guilt I felt when my sister got hurt on my watch when I was 10 or 11 years old. By putting myself in danger with these clients, I was trying to make up for what I felt I did back then to my sister. Geisler claimed I was always doing things out of guilt. As an example, a woman in my office got fired one week and she called me and asked to borrow some money. Even though she had borrowed money from me in the past without repaying it, I couldn't say no to her. He said I can never say no to anybody. He claimed

I get kicked in the ass time and time again by abusive people who I continue to try and please.

The doctor's notes indicated that I thought pressure was mounting on me. He said I didn't like the type of legal work I was doing anymore and I felt more on guard than ever. I started practicing law defensively, because every little thing I did was being documented. I was afraid that other clients would use something I told them to come back and bite me. The panel members asked him about the medications he prescribed for me, and how I reacted to them. All seemed to be going well and it looked like his description of me as a pretty stable guy would carry the day. Of course, the DDC had yet to cross examine him.

The DDC attorney then asked Dr. Geisler what seemed to be their most important question: If the client's allegations were true, would my conduct be related to my psychiatric condition? Geisler said there was no question in his mind that assuming the allegations were true, my allowing this to happen was part and parcel of allowing everyone to abuse me, whether it was a woman who was fired as a secretary in my office of simply one of my clients. Asked if there was a psychiatric explanation for my alleged conduct, the doctor answered, "Absolutely!" He said it was the guilt I felt over the injury suffered by my little sister when I was watching her; that I should have guarded her and kept her from having the accident.

"If you learned that Mr. Walters was the aggressor and had initiated some of the sexual contact with his client, would your opinion change?" asked the DDC attorney. "I don't think I could learn that," he said. "I don't think that's what happened." That wasn't at all what the DDC attorney wanted to hear and she decided to get a second opinion.

Under the rules of Professional Conduct in, after a Complaint has been filed the DDC has a right to have that attorney evaluated by a psychiatrist of their choosing. Prior to seeing their shrink, my attorney was ordered to present to their psychiatrist copies of all the Sworn Statements, depositions, complaints and replies. That means their doctor got to see my entire file. If it sounds unfair, it's because it is. It allows their psychiatrist to basically pre-judge his or her evaluation of me. According to the rules, I had no choice but to go along but it didn't make me any less furious.

Chapter 20

———————————

MY PSYCHE

I was sent to a Psychiatric Center whose specialty was review-ing matters that are involved in lawsuits. The Center gets a huge amount of business from the DDC and you can believe that unless they went along with the 'program,' they stood to lose a lot of business from the DDC. They were getting paid by the organization that was essentially asking them to find something wrong with their defendant. The appointment was scheduled four weeks in advance.

I sat next to a man in the waiting room who told me he was there because of a divorce case. Lawyers have a tendency to question people as if they were taking a deposition when hav-ing what most people would call a normal conversation. This is precisely what I did. I learned that his fists apparently got a little too frisky with a particular client and he tried to choke her at the same time. I didn't ask for any other details and started reading a magazine hoping that he wouldn't ask me about my situation.

I had to wait 45 minutes before my name was called. I was escorted into a cozy little room. Apart from a couch, the room was laced with flowers and contained enough decent looking art to indicate to me that my psychiatrist was something of an aficionado. His desk was clean and clear of clutter or documents. I surmised this wasn't a desk or office he used regularly and that he had examined my file in his real office. He came in about five minutes later.

"Hello, Mr. Walters. It's a pleasure to meet you," he said. "I'm Dr. Zwick. I've examined all the documents sent over by the DDC as well as the Deposition of Dr. Geisler and his reports. I know why you are here and I think that you and I will get along fine. I want to hear your side of the story and what you're all about so I can make a proper evaluation for the DDC."

We talked about my medical history before focusing on my law practice. He wanted to know about my relationship with my employees, particularly the female ones. We really didn't get into any specifics about my relationship to my client or her allegations. That would come in our second session, two weeks later. By then, I was a little more combative, disenchanted and worn out by this litigation. Not only was I working 12 hour days, but I received no support from anyone for what I was going through. I couldn't share it with others. The whole experience for me was terrifying, exhausting and expensive. Thank God I wasn't a drinker because that kind of habit could have made my situation a whole lot worse.

He asked me about the extent of my physical contact with Afshan. I said I found her attractive but also demanding and demeaning, as evidenced by her dramatic late night phone calls and unscheduled visits to my office. We talked about how I resisted her advances. I tried to avoid controversy or conflict, offering her my hand in friendship instead.

I told him she wanted to deny her husband his rights to see their children. In so doing, she had no legal ground to stand on. I'd always been taught that the visitation was for the good of the children and not for a client's own satisfaction. She rebuffed me every time I brought this up and I believe she attempted to seduce me in order to get me to come around to her point of view.

We talked about the litigation and what I thought about it. I candidly told him that I thought the DDC had overreacted, based on the evidence and the unreliability of my client. I suggested to him that they could have dismissed her allegations as sour grapes or even revenge. But, to disbar me and put a halt to my career and everything I had built would be an admission by them that my side of the story carried absolutely no weight. I couldn't buy that and I couldn't see how anyone else could, provided they were versed in this case.

My third office visit with Zwick was supposed to be my last. I was feeling that there might be some light at the end of the tunnel. I wasn't looking at the negatives anymore and didn't think he would bring some bias into his conclusions about me. We got along well and I kind of liked the guy. We had a good rapport and I felt I was very truthful with him. This was a big breakthrough for me, because I've always been a pessimist, which had no doubt contributed to my ongoing depression.

Zwick seemed to be his usual, jovial self as he entered the room. Attorneys tend to evaluate clients to determine whether or not they slept well the night before or if they appeared to have any problems. He asked me about my future and what changes I would make with my female clients if I continued to practice law.

I was ambivalent about what Zwick might say following our third and final session. I just wanted him to be fair. You never know what psychiatrists are thinking. You also never know if they can relate to what actually goes on in a law practice as volatile and dangerous as divorce. Dr. Zwick indicated to the court that the purpose of his evaluation was to perform an independent psychiatric examination and to determine whether or not there was psychiatric contradictions or if supervision was needed regarding me and my law practice. He said he performed a psychiatric evaluation on me and also evaluated psychological testings performed by his technician. He indicated that I had denied any past history of psychiatric illness or mental health treatment and that there was no family history of medical health problems. He described me as a workaholic, working 12 hour days, taking calls at home, and very rarely taking vacations.

Dr. Zwick explained that I had a long standing inability to say no to others and that my office staff would "push me around." He indicated that I denied any compromising of any of my work ethics because of any relationships with my employees. He thought I felt I needed to maintain good client relations with Afshan as well as others.

He substantiated Dr. Geisler's opinion that I was not really aware of being depressed. Over the last several years I was progressively becoming more socially withdrawn, pessimistic, and had a decreased inclination to engage in fun activities. I stopped doing household projects. He stated when I felt very stressed at work, I would "reward" myself by buying something or eating more. He noted I have less of a tendency now to "whine about my physical complaints."

Dr. Zwick concluded that I had prominent dependent personality traits, mild levels of depression and good reality testing. However, he stated that I had a tendency to distort my perceptions of situations to meet my own needs and that I may jump to hasty conclusions or over-value the relevant details when evaluating an interpersonal situation. He said I exhibited no prominent sociopathic traits.

Based on his evaluation, he agreed with Dr. Geisler's diagnosis that I suffered from dysthymic disorder. It was a chronic, mild depressive disorder which may cause a depressed mood, occasional difficulties with sleep, appetite, energy and motivation but does not significantly impair day-to-day functions. He said many people with dysthymia become so accustomed to feeling this way that they're not even aware they're depressed until they become involved in treatment or their condition improves.

Most important to me was that he said my dysthymic disorder had not had a major impact on my law practice. He said I was improving with treatment and saw no problem if I were to return to work. Despite having symptoms of the disease for years, he said I had been maintaining my practice very successfully. He said my profile wasn't similar to those frequently seen in sexual exploiters. This is probably the best statement he made because it showed that he considered my risk for future inappropriate sexual behavior was low. Thank God he came up with that. He strongly recommended continued therapy to deal with this issue.

I had no problem with continued physical therapy if it got me out of this situation. I had done nothing wrong and though I was somewhat perplexed by his report, I felt the overall conclusion was favorable enough that the DDC could sign-off on agreement that would be acceptable to them and not fatal to me. I wanted it over with.

Chapter 21

STOP THE COURT, WE'RE HAVING A BABY!

One of longest cases ever tried in New York County involved a carpenter. He was nailing something without protective eye coverings and the tip of the nail came off and flew into his eye. They took him to the hospital where they removed his eye. He got Nathan Osmond, the best lawyer in town, to represent him. Osmond spent more money than anybody did in those days. He spent one million dollars on this case, making metallurgical slides and photographs to show the jury that the broken nail wasn't made properly. I represented a hardware store that sold him the nail. They had no insurance so this trial was a make-or-break time for their business. Three other distributors were defendants and they had some of the best attorneys in New York representing them. The trial lasted 26 weeks.

During the trial's 16th week, my wife was ready to give birth to our first child. I called the judge and said he had to stop the trial, but he refused. I ended up calling him some names and he held me in contempt. I pissed him off so much that I got him up to 13 days in jail. I drove my wife to the hospital for my son's birth, after which I came back to the judge's chambers. I calmly told him his picture was most certainly going to be on the front page of the newspapers if he didn't vacate the contempt order against me. He saw the look in my eyes and didn't even try to argue with me. If he was upset, he sure didn't show it. I think I had shocked him so much that he thought I might be crazy. Before he vacated the order, he told the jurors that my wife had a baby and they all applauded. Because of that, the judge said I would be absent for the remainder of the morning. Because the jurors applauded, the other attorneys moved for a mistrial. They ended up arguing all morning which meant they didn't get any evidence in anyway.

When it was time for me to make a closing argument, the judge called me into his chambers. He told me the other lawyers on my team had taken a straw vote and they didn't want me to make a closing argument. They said they would take care of my closing argument in their closing argument. It was because I was a young lawyer and a little pisher. I said no, which was a pretty gutsy thing to do because my closing remarks were the dumbest arguments of my life. I said you people with glasses probably have worse eyesight than he does with just the one eye, and I kept driving that point home.

Holding a plastic eye, the plaintiff's lawyer said, "Take away his other eye and he is blind. In a world of blind people, the one-eyed man is king." The jury came back and awarded the plaintiff $50,000, far below what he was seeking. The firm representing him actually lost a great deal of money, because they spent a hell of a lot more money building their case than they ever got back.

I was trying to teach one of my firm's young attorneys how to make a closing argument and he thought he already knew how to do it. I went to the library and found a book entitled the Most Equitable Closing Arguments in the United States. I was thumbing through it and I stopped on the page that had my name on it. It was my closing argument from that case. The article said that I was held in contempt and that it was one of the most equitable closing arguments in the United States. To this day I can't remember what I said in my closing, but it was a WIN, WIN, WIN for me and a loss to his client. What I do remember is sitting there thinking I had never said anything more stupid in my entire life. It just goes to show you!

Chapter 22

DEPOSING THE STAFF

The DDC deposed my secretary of 14 years, Marsha Phillips. At 40, Marsha was very attractive; with makeup, she was a knockout. I had two other secretaries, but Marsha was the Office Manager. She was good at her job although we occasionally had our battles. At times we were like husband and wife and wouldn't talk to each other for a day or two. However, I would never have let her go and would have matched any offer she might receive from another firm. She kept the office together and made things run like a Swiss watch.

Like other firms, the entire staff had emotional ups and downs from time to time. The pressure in a law practice is constant and the phone calls never seem to stop. The client calls were not as problematic as they were emotionally abusive on each one of us. Many calls would begin with a client saying, "What the fuck are you going to do about my husband sending the children back with dirty clothes when I sent them to him with clean ones?" Marsha would spend time talking to these clients before the calls were transferred to me or the other lawyers. She was very effective at calming them down.

Marsha went over to Jeff Stone's office for her preparation. She didn't ask to talk to me before she went so she didn't have a clear understanding as to what her appearance was about. She later told me that when she got to Stone's office, he went right for the jugular by asking if there had ever been any sexual relations between me and her. She said there hadn't been. He asked her about advances made by me, sexual overtures, and if she ever observed them in the office.

There was a time when you could tell a secretary that her hair looked nice or that she wore a pretty dress, or that she looked cute. You can't do that today, and it causes a fair amount of office tension. In my firm, you could have cut the air with a knife. Everybody was walking on eggshells, aware that anything they said to a fellow employee might come back at them as a sexual pass.

After her deposition, I reviewed the transcript and was content with the answers that Marsha gave. She said she was present during many of my conversations with female clients. She said the doors to my office were so thin you could hear my loud voice even when they were closed. She said there were never any rumors or gossip around the office that I was making passes or being flirtatious with other female employees.

Q. Have you ever had an interest in him, romantically?
A. No, none whatsoever.

Q. And why is that?

A. I certainly did not find him attractive.

Q. Did any of the clients regularly complain to you.

A. Of course they did. This was a divorce practice and all they did was complain, vent and bitch. I mean, they were not the most sophisticated people on this earth. It could get to you. We never are doing enough for them. No matter what we did, there were complaints, constantly, all day, with every phone call and they were very abusive.

Q. I mean, did they complain about Mr. Walters' making sexual advances or being flirtatious with them.

A. No, never!

Q. Regarding the client in question, did you ever see him in any manner unprofessional to her, including an informal, casual, sexual type relationship.

A. No.

Q. Did you ever see the client leave the office with his arm around her?

A. No.

Q. Did you receive any phone calls from the client that went directly to him?

A. Yes.

Q. Did you screen the calls before you gave the calls to him?

A. I always do.

Q. When you screened the calls from this particular client, did the client say anything unusual to indicate there was more than a professional relationship between Mr. Walters and her?

A. No.

Q. Did you ever find him irritated when the client called?

A. Yes, she irritated everybody in the office, not just him. There were times when she came in unexpectedly and made a scene. She would yell and scream on the telephone before I was able to transfer the calls to him. She was an obnoxious individual as far as I can remember. We have many of those type of clients.

Q. Did Mr. Walters ever explain to you what type of litigation was going on between this client and himself and the DDC?

A. Yes, he had an office meeting with everybody and briefly explained to us what was happening.

Q. Did he or his attorneys tell you what to say today before the deposition in answer to any of our questions?

A. No.

Marsha kept her answers to a brief yes or no as much as she could and she told the truth. As far as I was concerned, she was one hell of a witness.

Chapter 23

IT RUNS IN THE FAMILY

I was an advertising guy at heart. It stimulated my creative side in a way that nothing had before. I came up with an idea for a famous Green Giant campaign. There were peas out in a field and the peas were freezing, because they were pouring sauce on them and locking the favor in. So, the peas elected someone to represent them and that person went to the Green Giant offices, knocked on the door, and said, "We have a problem. We don't want you to keep freezing us by throwing butter sauce all over us and locking the flavor in." The campaign ran for quite some time on television. I think my life would have been measurably happier if I had stuck to advertising. However, I got married, had children, bought a house and needed some more money to support my family. It wasn't possible for me to switch occupations, so I ended up hating the practice of law and dreaded every day that I went to work.

Both of my siblings were lawyers and both have children who are attorneys. I'm the only one who handled family law. My brother and sister were passionate about the law, but I wasn't. It just wasn't my cup of tea. However, owing to New York's patronage system, I became a part-time assistant Attorney General, during which time I was directed to open up the vault of a famous celebrity after he died. This was routine procedure by the government who wanted to make sure they got their fair share of what was owed them by the celebrity's estate. If Al Capone's secret vault had contents anywhere near as valuable as what we found in that celebrity's vault, they'd still be talking about the haul today. I had three men working for me and the time at it took three days to finish going through the things that we found.

Early in my career, I started taking jury cases rather than non-jury cases. Jury cases can take a couple of weeks. Non-jury cases take about an hour and are continued to another date, at which time it takes another hour, and so on and so on. That's how that works. Jury cases are very difficult and there was one year when I tried more cases than all but a handful of attorneys in this county.

I used to refer clients to my sister for years but I eventually stopped doing it because of a lack of reciprocity. My relationship with her was never very close but I considered her to be my friend. Whenever she had a major problem, I would always help her as much as I could. We were just so different. I offered her a job at my firm but she didn't take it. She made her own way and was very successful. We generally talked only when there family matters that needed our attention.

Years later, my little sister died of cancer. I miss her dearly. I always go back to the time when she was injured on my watch. She stayed in my heart from that day on. Because our birthdays were on the same day, I feel empty now on my birthday. My instinct is to call her but, of course, I know I can't.

Chapter 24

ORANGES TO PUMPKINS

I was going deeper into depression because there seemed to be no end in sight. The DDC attorney reminded me of a person who makes up her mind in advance and works backward, trying to justify her decision in spite of the facts. I found her callousness to be reprehensible. I was almost at the end of my rope when something happened to divert attention away from me and my case.

A well-known, high-priced divorce attorney named Jack Leamington got caught having a continuing sexual relationship with a client. He had secretly taken a video of the two of them in bed together. To make things worse, he continued to bill his client for the time they spent in bed. His actions had a major impact on my case. His record with the DDC was public and I was able to extract other information from it.

When this woman came to Leamington seeking a divorce, he made several passes at her and they went out to dinner on three separate occasions. After the last dinner, Leamington was driving his client home when he convinced her that she could have an extra-marital affair. He told her that committing adultery wouldn't be "considered" in a distribution of any of the couple's assets. He said it would be like a no fault divorce, meaning it didn't matter who caused the divorce and what they did. The assets would still be distributed fairly or 50-50.

They went to an inexpensive Bronx motel, so that no one would recognize him. It had to be in a low-income neighborhood and had to be a motel where he could pay cash instead of using a credit card. Leamington was married and didn't want a paper trail for his shenanigans. He kept both a digital camera and compact video camera in the trunk of his car at all times. He planned to video any sexual activity he had with his client and took the camera out of his trunk and concealed it in his briefcase which he brought into the room. When she went to the bathroom, he set the video camera up on a dresser across from the bed. He managed to camouflage it so it wasn't readily noticeable.

Leamington taped their entire episode. After they got out of bed, she went into the bathroom again and he placed the video camera back into his briefcase. His client was unaware of his use of the camera until she discovered it at what turned out to be their last sexaul encounter. She was appalled, surprised and scared. Leamington said he had intended to ask her permission to tape their activities but never found the opportune time to do so. His client knew he was lying.

She told the DDC that most of their sexual escapades were secretly videoed by him. When the DDC made a formal request that the videos be produced, Leamington had no choice but to admit that there were videos because she had seen the camera. Questions in the Sworn Statement produced 75 pages of transcripts and were highly revealing.

Q. Before you got out of the vehicle and went into the motel office, you took the video camera out of the truck of your car with the intent to do what?
A. I felt it was a consensual relationship and that it would be consensual to video it.
Q. Previously, you testified that she had no knowledge that she was being videoed?
A. Yes.
Q. What was the intent of videoing it. I mean, what were you going to use the video for?
A. It's nice to look at these videos with your partner before you have intimacy, because it could turn both of you on.
Q. Well, that leads me to the next question. How many times have you done this before the first time you went to a motel with your client?
A. Maybe once or twice.
Q. The times that you did it "once or twice," were they also with clients?
A. No.
Q. Who were they with?

A. Just other friends.

Q. Were these 'other friends' prostitutes, acquaintances, social friends or what?

A. One was a prostitute and the other was a social friend.

Q. After you got into the motel room on the first time you went, what took place after you closed the door?

A. I took the bottle of wine I had in my briefcase out and poured us each a glass and she sat on the chair and I sat on the bed and we talked.

Q. What did you talk about?

A. Well, I think we both had intimacy on our minds and I was hoping to establish that we both wanted to participate.

Q. How long did you talk?

A. Approximately 20 minutes or so.

Q. Did you have any food in addition to the wine?

A. No.

Q. After the 20 minutes what took place?

A. She came and sat on the bed across from me and we talked a little further.

Q. What took place next?

A. The left arm that was supporting her sitting on the bed dropped down, but before it did she handed me the empty glass she had. I got up from the bed and put her glass and my glass on the dresser and sat back down on the bed. I bent down and kissed her.

Q. Did you kiss her on the lips?

A. Yes.

Q. What did you do next?

A. We made out in a fashion and I began to lay next to her.

Leamington's statement went on and on as to each step of the sexual encounter. No embarrassing detail was off the table to the DDC lawyer. The DDC had the goods on Leamington. They had the tape and had learned he had a history of going out with his clients. This behavior, of course, was completely contrary to what my story was all about. Most important, the case against Jack Leamington was going to have a huge impact on mine.

As I reviewed the legal documents in Jack Leamington's case, it became clear that the DDC knew he had sexual encounters with more than one client. He first denied having any relationship with any client, but he recanted and claimed he couldn't be charged with perjury because it was consensual and fell within the protected zone of privacy. Even though his statements were untrue, he argued that they weren't material, and therefore, no perjury in his DDC testimony was possible. The DDC said the activity was not consensual and cited an example that his arguments about materiality would mean that he could actually rape a client, lie about it before the DDC, and then claim the sexual conduct was within a zone of privacy protected by the United States Constitution.

The DDC disagreed with Leamington's premise. They cited cases claiming that the Supreme Court had the inherent power to regulate the practice of law and to create disciplinary proceedings. They said the case that Leamington had cited involved malpractice and that the Appellate Court had noted that the lawyer's behavior in that case may have been unethical, but it did not rise to the level of malpractice. They maintained that it's impossible to identify and state in a code, statute or rule, every conceivable situation where discipline may be appropriate. Therefore, they said, discipline may be imposed for "engaging in conduct which tends to bring the Courts or legal profession into disrepute, for conduct prejudicial to the administration of justice, or for failure to withdraw from employment when his professional judgment on behalf of a client may be affected by his own personal interests."

In the main case against him, Leamington had told his client to say "yes" to whatever questions were asked of her while on the witness stand. He phrased the questions in a way to show that she had approved the Settlement Agreement with her ex-husband. A few other women had filed Complaints against him and the DDC sought to contact each one of them. They were all clients that he took to a motel or to their own place for sex. He was extremely aggressive and had established a pattern of making sexual advances to women he felt sexually attracted to. All the while I'm thinking how different and egregious Leamington's behavior was, compared to what I had been charged with. They had no video or taped conversations between me and my clients. All the DDC had was her word in what amounted to a 'he said, she said' scenario.

Leamington had a fine reputation in the legal community as a high-end divorce lawyer. I gave him a call. "Jack," I said, "you don't know me, but I'm the other case that's going on with the

DDC and I think we should sit down and see if we can help each other." He agreed to see me and we met at a secluded spot in the back of a restaurant, which at our 4 p.m. meeting was almost empty. He was around 6'2", appeared to carry a few extra pounds, and showed signs of wear and tear in his face. He was about my age but, unlike me, had managed to hold onto most of his hair. We exchanged greetings and sat down. I took no notes because I didn't want to give him any cause for alarm.

I told him I had been involved in litigation for more than two years and I wondered if we could 'team up' to help each other. He admitted he had consulted with his own attorneys about my case and had reviewed the public document. The main similarity in our cases was the fact that there were no laws, statutes or any case history that prevented an attorney from having consensual sexual contact with any of their clients. His case was different than mine because there were videos, aggressive behavior on his part and more than one woman was involved. He had also repeatedly engaged in sexual intercourse with several clients while I had only resisted the sexual advances of one of my clients.

We talked for about an hour and explored every possible way that we could help each other. We talked about some of the Constitutional provisions that he had cited in his pleadings and some of the case law from other jurisdictions that would help both of us. We also talked about the political maneuvering by the prosecuting attorney whose goal was to climb the ladder of success as quickly as possible. We realized there was little we could accomplish, other than to exchange the research that our attorneys has prepared. I felt he was going to go down the river with more than a suspension.

He was going to be disbarred. Knowing that, I realized I could be railroaded and maybe I shouldn't chance it. Instead, I should probably take a plea and accept a suspension, with a stay of the suspension, and a year of psychiatric help. All of a sudden, I thought I got a glimpse of the light at the end of the tunnel.

Jack Leamington saved my ass. Comparing his sexual misconduct with mine, was like comparing oranges to pumpkin seeds. The circumstances of the two cases were as different as night and day, at least the way I looked at it. Making their case against me was really a stretch and was only attempted because they had no other outlet to pursue. Leamington basically gave them all they needed and did so on a silver platter.

Even my own client admitted that I never asked her out, never dated her, never took her any place for a romantic adventure, didn't have dinner with her, didn't come up to her place, didn't send her flowers, didn't video us having sex, and didn't have any evidence of communication with her that showed a sexual relationship. The DDC had all of that with Leamington's case plus he was still billing her. His was an open and shut case. Mine was anything but.

My attorney was now in a position to negotiate some type of settlement of this matter with the DDC. The Leamington case would allow the DDC attorney to make her name with the press and would certainly have a larger impact in the legal industry. If my client persisted in pursuing a case against me, the DDC attorney would have to go all the way to the Court of Appeals, there would be a trail and a lot of doubt as to whether or not I was guilty. Bingo! My attorney Jeff Stone apparently thought the same thing when he heard about Leamington's case. He called me and we discussed how we could use his case to our advantage. Stone asked me what kind of consequences I could tolerate to make my case go away. There were several factors I needed to consider.

I had paid a small fortune in fees to the attorneys on my case and I needed to stop the financial bleeding. I was politely informed by Stone that I would also be responsible for all the expenses of the DDC because that's part of the New York statute. I reluctantly agreed with Stone to let him negotiate some kind of way out of this predicament for me. Weeks went by and as the case against Leamington got stronger, my case became less important. The DDC prosecutor, Barbara Goldman, reduced her demand of disbarment to a one-year suspension and no therapy. Our counter offer was no suspension with one year of therapy.

As more weeks went by, the case against Leamington got even stronger. I became an "unimportant aspect" to Goldman which is the only reason she agreed to have meaningful negotiations with my attorney. My attorney negotiated a settlement where I would be suspended for one month, with a stay of the suspension, if I would see a psychiatrist at least twice a month for a year. The suspension would be lifted if I completed the psychiatric visits. I would be monitored by a probation office.

When Jeff Stone called me with the news, my heart dropped. I was relieved but not entirely happy. Why give in, I thought. The case should have never been brought against me in the first place. I could take the case to the Court of Appeals and my chances of winning were at least 80%. I didn't rape anybody. I didn't take advantage of anybody. I'm not a pedophile or a sexual predator so why would I voluntarily take such a punishment?

In a word, money. I was not a wealthy man. I had to take out some loans to pay my lawyers. Then there was the problem of my reputation which had already been extremely damaged in the eyes of my wife, my children and the legal community. Also, I'm sure I would be cited in any new statute that the DDC prosecutor would recommend to the State Legislature. On the negative side, I had to at least allow for the possibility that Leamington might be vindicated entirely, a situation which would put me back in the DDC's crosshairs.

My attorney made the deal. The Consent Petition stated that the DDC was recommending that I be suspended for a period of 30 days and that the suspension be "stayed" and that I be placed on probation for a period of one year during which time I would continue to receive psychiatric help. The DDC felt the stayed suspension, with probation, would adequately protect the public and be consistent with decisions from other jurisdictions.

However, the DDC made sure that each and every thing I had ever been charged with, or was thought to have done, was included in sections of the agreement. It claimed that the evidence would establish by clear and convincing proof that I had engaged in the following misconduct:

Overreaching.

Failure to withdraw from employment when my professional judgment on behalf of the client was affected by my own personal interests.

Conduct which tends to defeat the administration of justice or bringing the Court or the legal profession into disrepute in violation of Supreme Court rules.

In part III, "Description of Respondent's Mitigation Evidence," it stated I had not previously been subject to discipline and that I had undergone weekly psychotherapy and had been evaluated by their own psychiatrist. The diagnosis was severe depression, with obsessive-compulsive tendencies and that this all occurred during my representation of this particular client. It further indicated that the psychiatrist had prescribed anti-depressant medication which I was taking and that it was unlikely that I would be harmful to the public if I continued practicing law during this period of rehabilitation.

I was ordered to reimburse the Commission for the costs of the proceedings and reimburse the DDC for any further costs incurred during the course of the probation. Probation would be revoked if I was found to have violated any of its terms. Probation would terminate after one year without further order if I complied with all the terms of the Settlement Agreement.

I was exhausted. I didn't want to get hung up in Leamington's case and I knew if I continued with my own case, I would be cited in his case and his case was going to be publicized a hell of a lot more than mine was. The bottom line was that the public would never even know what had taken place with my case unless they had inquired with the DDC. I would not have to lose one day of work as an attorney with this type of final agreement. I wasn't going to be disbarred, nor was I going to be dragged through the mud with Leamington's case. Would this mean I got my life back? I'm afraid it wasn't going to be that easy. What was waiting for me down the road was both unbelievable and terrifying.

Chapter 25

UNDERSTANDING JUDGES

I never wanted to sit on the Bench. Judges have to be at events with lawyers three or four nights a week. They generally mix very well and favors are always passed out at these get-togethers. Judges need to dress well and be clean shaven all the time. They don't all do it, but they should because judges have to set a consistent example to the public. I'm not in favor of wearing a suit after leaving work, but it's one of those things you need to do if you sit on the Bench. Judges get respect on the street, but generally the respect ends once they leave the legal district. So, what's the point of being a judge? In a word, POWER.

Lawyers are lawyers because they want power. Cops are cops because they want power. I believe the same is true, or even truer, of most judges, politicians and doctors, too. You might be surprised to learn that it's always the lawyer who controls things in court, not the judge. We pretend the judge wrote the jury instructions. What really happens is that two lawyers hand the judge 25 pages of instructions for the jury. He rules on their admissibility, but we draw them up. We make our motions in chambers before our closing arguments, and those negotiations can get downright nasty.

Sometimes the system makes no sense whatsoever. A guy I know became a judge 10 years ago in spite of having a very bad history in the courts. He once punched a lawyer and was handcuffed and ushered into the judge's chambers to cool down. He also had a reputation of lying to other lawyers and created a toxic atmosphere by pushing people around whenever he could. He once got in front of a jury to make a closing argument and the judge warned him not to use the word "insurance". So, this lawyer said the word three times in front of the jury. The judge said he was going to hold him in contempt and the guy said, "You don't know how to do that, I do, nobody else does, I do. And I'm not gonna write the order to hold myself in contempt."

At any given time, there are numerous complaints from dissatisfied clients that the Judge had made sexual advances towards them. Because of that, new rules are in place that prohibit attorneys from bringing their clients into the Judge's chambers for pre-trial conferences with opposing counsel. Numerous allegations have been made by clients against Judges that were ludicrous and totally false, but all such allegations have to be investigated. It had really gotten out of hand by the time they changed the rule.

A client's wife was constantly calling me, saying I was crooked and that she was going to kill me. During my client's divorce trial, I put her on the stand and asked the judge to search her for weapons. The judge said in open court that I wasn't Dick Tracy and if I wanted my name in the newspaper, there were other ways to do it. I asked the woman on the stand what her name was, for the record, and she blurted out that the judge was crooked and no good. The judge immediately called for the bailiffs to search the woman, thus exonerating me on my motives for saying what I did. This judge later became a Supreme Court Justice in the state of New York. Turns out this guy knew how to get his name in the newspaper.

A judge worked out with me at the gym for awhile and I told him I wasn't going to call him Judge anymore. When he asked why, I told him it was because he was my friend. He appreciated it and he encouraged other people to start calling him by his first name. He liked it because he knew those people were his friends. The way I see it, judges are just like you and me, only more insecure.

Ten years ago, women started to manipulate the courts by saying their husbands were molesting their daughters. It was an attempt to get the judge to deny visitation. Now the allegations are so prevalent that 2 out of 5 women allege child molestation. The result was that everyone must go see a psychiatrist now. You can no longer expect judges to side with you based solely on those types of allegations.

There was a judge by the name of Jack Feldman who asked the lawyers to approach the bench without their clients. He'd say, "Does one of you have to be a screamer to impress your client?" If one of the attorneys said yes, he'd instruct the other one not to interrupt the screaming, after which we'd go into chambers and talk seriously. He would always ask the clients if they slept together the night before. If they said yes, he would say, "Sorry, I'm not divorcing you today. I'll give you a continuance for a couple of months. If you can stay away from each other that long, then I'll divorce you. If you jump in bed with each other, you can't tell me you want a divorce. Not in this lifetime."

Judges can make you laugh. A mother goes to court and says her ex-husband only feeds the kids pizza for six weeks. Judge says there's nothing wrong with that because pizza has a lot of vitamins. Bada bing! One judge devised a unique decision on visitation which he considered to be a proper one. He had the wife move in for three days, then she had to leave and the husband moved in for four days. Bada Bing! Unfortunately, that didn't work. In the legal system, sometimes things don't work out the way they should but sometimes, thank God they do.

Chapter 26

ANOTHER MARRIAGE IN PERIL

I sat in my car in our driveway with the motor running, pondering what a relief it was to have ended the proceedings against me. Seeing the psychiatrist was not a problem and was, in fact, the greatest relaxation I ever had. I didn't have to make any decisions when I was talking to him. All he had to do was listen without having to make any snap decisions.

As I got out of my car, another vehicle pulled up to my driveway. I approached the car to see who it was and the driver asked me if I was Mr. Walters. When I said I yes, he handed me a few pieces of paper. He was a process server and he served me with divorce papers. Well, if it wasn't one thing, it was another. For two hours, I had the feeling that this long nightmare had finally been put behind me. Yes, my legal career had been saved, but now my marriage was on life support. I didn't expect this at all, but I probably should have.

All the piss and vinegar had been taken out of me. I let the process server leave without making any sarcastic comment and that wasn't like me. I felt like a balloon whose air was slowly being drained. I went into the house hoping my wife was out so I could reflect on this new circumstance in peace. However, she was there. I asked her if she wanted to talk about the divorce with me. "I'd be glad to sit down with you to discuss where we're going with this," she said.

I felt myself starting to tighten up. The heaviness I had felt for all but the last two hours returned with a vengeance. "You know I love you," I said to her. She said she understood that but the divorce proceedings were something that "had to be." All I said was, "Why?" She said she understood what the DDC was doing, even though I had tried to keep her in the dark. She had friends who were lawyers and had asked them a lot of questions so she could put all the pieces together. For my part, I tried to downplay the circumstances of the proceedings against me as trivial.

"Greg, I have been ridiculed by all my friends," she said painfully. "I have had to defend you in the neighborhood as well as amongst our friends. I didn't know all the facts, but I defended you. I did my best to keep a straight face and not break down each and every time someone asked me about your situation. I could never understand why you would have relations with another woman when we had such a good life together. The bullshit of you being seduced never flew with me, or anybody else for that matter. Gossip is gossip, but everybody, and I mean everybody, thinks you have been a womanizer all your life. No one has any specifics, but that is your general reputation.

"Have I fallen out of love with you? The answer is no. Do I like you? The answer is no. I can't possibly be content any longer because of the stigma that is attached to you - and now me. If you're late coming home, I'll never really know if you're with another woman. This will always be going through my head and I can't possibly trust you anymore. I feel my only option now is to get a divorce and to try to get over this stigma. It continues to affect me and our children. You can't possibly imagine what they are going through with their friends and the ridicule they've been subjected to. I can only imagine that when they're in school, one of their so-called friends will be saying, 'Your father fucks his clients.'"

It's difficult to get much lower than I felt at that moment. Ever feel like you totally failed your wife and children? God, I hope not. I felt like I was facing another prosecuting attorney and that the trial was already on. The difference was that my wife wasn't trying to get me. She had a strong case and my case was feeble at best. She was doing what she felt she had to do, and I don't begrudge her that for a second. That being said, I knew that the presentation I was about to make to my wife had better be the finest closing argument I had ever given. A lot more than money and my legal reputation was at stake here. I felt like I was on the verge of losing my family and that made me feel worse than anything that had ever happened to me. I know it's a cliche, but I had apparently gone from the frying pan into the fire. I did not deserve it and I was not going down without a fight.

"Honey, today we wrapped up my case. I was going to tell you when I got home tonight that our problems are 99% over. I wasn't disbarred. I can still make a living at what I do best. Yes, I created this problem, I won't deny that. The hell that I went through the last couple of years and the money I spent in defending myself has taken its toll on me as well as you. I'm not asking you to feel my pain. Has this experience affected how I feel about you? No. I love you dearly and I want to save our marriage. Why not pick up the pieces and repair the damage, instead of throwing away our entire lives and making it more difficult for the children?

"I'm not the cause of this. There are no excuses I need to make and I'm not guilty. Yes, I'm guilty of putting myself in this situation and I'm guilty of putting you and the kids through this. This is not my doing, but I think we can salvage our marriage and make it stronger. Can't we just put the divorce on a holding pattern before I hire an attorney to defend myself? I would like you to reconsider what you're doing. Call me if I'm late coming home. I always have my cell phone with me and you know I'm so crazy that I always answer every call, even the ones from deranged clients. I've never not answered a call from you and I never will. The bottom line is that I love you very much and I want this trouble to go away. I want it to be a joint decision by both of us to attempt to work it out. It takes two to tango and I can't make this better unless we both want it to get better. Help me out, honey. Give me a break. I love you very much."

With that, she walked away and went upstairs to our bedroom. "If you wish, I'll sleep downstairs tonight," I said. "I don't think that's necessary," she replied. My eyes kind of lit up with hope and I wanted to believe that she really meant it. But, I just didn't know. We slept as far away from each other as we could in our queen bed. I couldn't fault her for being cold with me. I couldn't fault her for anything. There were no words of substance spoken by either of us and it was one of the longest nights of my life.

The following day I left early, as I always do, and she was still sleeping. It was a Monday and a stack of mail was waiting for me. There was a letter from the Federal District Court that I hadn't expected. They informed me that my admission to practice law in the Federal Courts of the United Stated had been revoked as of the date of the "Discipline on Consent." It could be reinstated if I successfully completed my probation period and observed all the conditions required of me. We didn't have many federal cases each year but the impact and the effect it could have on my reputation caused me to be startled and surprised by the letter.

There was also another letter from the New York Bar Association informing me that I was no longer to receive referrals from their Hire an Attorney Service. It felt like a double whammy. Depression descended upon me like it had when the protective order to bar my name from the proceedings was rejected by the Supreme Court. I refrained from calling my wife to vent, thinking that sympathy from her to me was probably in very short supply.

I got through the morning and decided to call my wife to tell her where we were in the ball game. I was surprised that she was home when I called. I would have preferred she not answer the phone. I told her about the two letters I had received and how I felt about them. Then I asked her if she had given any more thought to our predicament. She said she had, but hadn't come to any conclusions. I told her how important I thought it was for her to take her time. The fact that she kept her responses to one or two words told me she wasn't in the mood to talk. I asked her if we could go out to dinner and have a nice evening together, but she flatly said no. I backed off knowing that I had absolutely no control over her responses or feelings. The ball was definitely in her court.

My attorney explained he still had to work out the probation details with the Probation Officer of the DDC and there were also a few other little matters to attend to before completing the entire process. Then he mentioned that I still owed his firm $75,000. I assured him I would pay this debt in monthly installments of $10,000 and he had no problem with that. He told me he knew the two letters I received would be coming but saw no good reason to tell me, given everything I had to deal with. I told him my wife had served me with divorce papers. He was very sympathetic with me and thought my wife and I could work things out.

I came home earlier than usual that night to avoid being criticized for being late. We sat down for dinner. After a few minutes she said, "You know, we have to tell the children." I said we should do it together but not until we exhausted all possibilities of there being a reconciliation. "Let's take this slowly so we can both think about where we're going and what the impact of this will be on all of us." She agreed. I felt so guilty that I started to help with the dishes and kitchen clean up. This was something I normally didn't do and the smile on her face was nothing if not ironic. Ironic is a good word because the sucker punch hasn't come yet.

Chapter 27

WON'T GET FOOLED AGAIN

I was trying to let the dust settle on my life when my secretary got a call from Afshan. The woman who had filed the Complaint with the DDC, the person who had tried to ruin my life and had put me into debt defending myself against her made up charges, wanted to make an appointment with me. Go figure. She told my secretary I shouldn't be in fear of calling her because she still respected my judgment and that's why she was seeking my advice. It was the last thing I would have expected and she was the last person I wanted to deal with.

I knew I'd have to be totally nuts to even return her call. The problem was that I couldn't help wondering what she wanted to talk about. I wanted to find that out just to satisfy my own curiosity. Maybe she would confess to her lies. I called my attorney and told him about the call. He said I would be absolutely crazy to make an appointment with her and if I did, he wanted no part of it. He said he was going to send me a "protect your ass" letter which would put on the record that he had recommended that I do not call her back or communicate with her in any way, shape, form or fashion.

I felt I needed to feed my curiosity. I planned on just listening to her and I called her. She said her husband had a new girlfriend who he brought with him on his visitation days. His girlfriend was trying to get the children to call her Mommy. "Why did you call me?" I asked. "Believe it or not, I had all the confidence in the world in you," she said. "I was always able to talk to you and you always gave me the proper advice. I panicked when you told me that I must allow him to see the children."

I got the feeling that she wanted to tell me she had been wrong in making up the stories she told the DDC. However, she couldn't get the words out of her mouth because she knew she would be in trouble if she did. I told her I would call her back. Against the advice of my attorney and against everything I knew to be true, I decided to have her come into the office for a meeting. I just had to know her motive behind all that had happened. Yes, I was foolish, very foolish, but I wanted to find out what made her tick. We set up an appointment for the following Monday at 2 p.m. I made sure the door remained open at all times and that there was a secretary within hearing distance outside my doorway. I knew if I had a third person in the room with us, the chances of her being honest with me were reduced even further.

She came in and sat down. I showed no contempt or anger towards her. I wanted to act professionally so there would be no hesitation on her part to talk to me, if, in fact, she wanted to talk to me. We talked about her new problem and what, if anything, could be done to resolve it. Her ex-husband was obviously trying to establish a bond between his girlfriend and the children. As we became more relaxed with each other in the conversation, I stopped talking and asked, "Why?" She knew what I was talking about. She said she lied about making the first advance towards me and seducing me. It seemed like she dropped her guard. She said she got vicious when I told her she must let him see the children. She wasn't going to let me or anybody else dictate to her how much visitation he was going to have, if any, and that she was going to be the controlling factor throughout the relationship after the divorce was final. She said I had painted her into a corner and left her no options. Deep down in her heart she knew I was right and there was no way out for her. The only way out was for her to stall everything and the way to do that was to report me to the DDC.

She had made the decision early on that as punishment, she wasn't going to let her ex-husband see the children. She admitted to me that she was very vindictive. The only way she could avoid the inevitable was to make sexual advances to me and hope I took the bait. This all made sense to me but I had the nagging feeling that there she may have had a hidden motive. She caused a great amount of damage to my career, my family and my future. Part of me knew I should be venting my animosity toward her and nobody would have faulted me for doing so. Instead, like a dummy, I merely conversed with her when I shouldn't have even been in the same room with her.

The question now became whether I should go back to the DDC through my attorney and try to reverse everything that had taken place, based on what she just told me. But, if I did, could I go through the trauma of litigation again? I'd have to spend more money in attorney fees, that much was sure. There would have to be another investigation, another complaint would be filed and there would be more hearings, at which it's unlikely she would admit to having our conversation. It could take a year or longer and I'd have to be very careful of any bad publicity that might bring this matter to the attention of the public.

As it stood now, the publicity about my case had almost totally died down. I had problems with my own divorce looming and trying to get my law practice up to speed again. I was getting dangerously close to putting myself in the kind of place where nervous breakdowns go to happen. I realized I would be better off leaving things the way they were and complete the terms of my suspension.

I needed to be careful so as to not mislead her into thinking I would again be her attorney. I told her this in no uncertain terms. Because of our past problems with the DDC, I told her I could no longer represent her, now or in the future. I referred her to my friend, Jake Powers, whose practice was similar to mine. He's a compassionate guy and though he understood what she had done to me, he agreed to take her case. You're probably thinking there's a sucker born every minute, and I'm sure there is. But, just because I let Afshan run her nasty little scheme on me, doesn't mean all she has to do is bat her eyes a few times and show a little cleavage to cast a spell on an unsuspecting attorney.

Knowing Jake, he'd have my client figured out before she even sat down to discuss her case.

I was relieved when she left my office. I hoped that I would never again see her, hear her voice or receive any correspondence from her. I had more important matters to consider. All day long I had been pondering what to tell our children. I'd given advice to hundreds of divorce clients but now it finally hit home and frankly, I didn't know what to do. Should I tell the children the details of the litigation with the DDC? Should I tell them their mom and I are seeking our own paths because of other factors? Is there any way to soften the blow? Do I make my wife look like the bad guy? No, that last option is no option at all because for one thing, it wouldn't be truthful. It would just give my wife another reason to resent me, and make me look and feel like more of a loser than I already did.

I pondered this matter all day long. I was going to tell my kids the truth but I needed to clear my head before doing so. I had a great deal of hope that my wife was going to make every attempt to reconcile and hold off on the divorce to allow me to win back her trust and confidence. Unfortunately, I had no control of anything anymore, nor did I deserve it.

I decided to have a serious conversation with my wife prior to speaking with our children. Until now, her attitude had been that she needed to get divorced from me and I should support her decision. She was 80% sure of this. We decided to talk about it at a restaurant at 10 p.m. so we could talk undisturbed. We went to Maxine's, a boutique deli that catered to the Jewish population. We both looked at the menu uncomfortably. I ordered coffee and a small piece of sugarless pie. She ordered a Cobb salad, a move that showed me she was more relaxed than I was. After placing our orders, I told her my bottom line was that I didn't want us to get divorced, that I still loved her dearly and very much wanted to save our marriage. I had repeated these things many times over the last few weeks but she told me she didn't know if she could ever trust me again. I assured her that our children were old enough to deal with our situation. Thousands of people get divorced every year and their children usually don't go off the deep end. They learn to manage and continue with life as it is. This was a matter of establishing that we had so much to lose if we broke up, and so much to gain if we stayed together. "Let's try it for a six-month probationary period or the like," I said.

She talked about how cold our relationship was now, both emotionally and sexually. She always had in the back of her mind that I was a depressed individual whose cup was always half empty. "If there ever was a pessimist, it's you," she said. I couldn't argue with her because she was right. I am a depressed person. Not depressed enough to consider suicide, but depressed enough to go to sleep very early, to not enjoy life or have any fun, or to participate in anything that was enjoyable. I always had excuses as to why I couldn't do anything outside of the house. Even going to a baseball game was a hassle for me. My wife knew all of this long before the psychiatrists made their diagnoses. She said she was an optimistic person, but that I tore her down for that as much as I possibly could.

She had talked to her friends, her brother and her parents. My in-laws didn't want to take sides, but her brother did. He told her he could see our lives were pretty miserable even before the litigation, and he was right. He spoke his mind and was understandably hard on me. I told my wife what I told all of my clients; that the only way to save a marriage was to continue living together. Experimenting with a separation and living apart tends to make things worse for a relationship in crisis.

She told me that I needed to retain an attorney and/or make a settlement proposal to her because she wanted out of our marriage. She said she wanted the house with all of its equity going to her and a 50-50 split of the rest of our assets. She wanted me out of the house within 60 days and would make a list of what furniture she wanted. She would leave it up to the attorneys to work out the particulars of child support, maintenance, my pension and other related matters. She assumed I was going to get an attorney because she knew that a lawyer who represents himself has a fool for a client.

Let her have what she wants, I thought to myself. My God, she deserves at least half of everything because she provided me with a wonderful life and children, and was a terrific wife. This was her choice and her wish and I really didn't want to fight anymore. I was completely drained from the litigation. I was also feeling sorry for myself. I had been under siege for a long time and now the chickens were coming home to roost. There are moments in life when a person feels totally defeated and helpless to do anything about it. That's the feeling I had as I listened to my wife tell me she was done with me.

We decided to tell the children the following day at 6 p.m. and invited them to come to our house. Donna and I agreed we would tell them that we both wanted to move on with our lives separately. Staying with each other was stifling our personal objectives. We still loved each other and didn't want to blame each other or anyone else for us wanting to divorce. I felt a little more depressed leaving the restaurant that I did going in. I felt even worse by the time we got to the car. We didn't say a word to each other on the drive home. We were both exhausted and had heavy hearts. Neither one of us was looking forward to the conversation we planned on having with our kids.

Chapter 28

AFTER LAW SCHOOL

I never thought I'd be an attorney, nor did I ever want to be one. The only reason I went to law school was to get out of the Army. I started working for a law firm out of law school. I was there a week when a cop ordered me to pull over on a downtown street. I wasn't breaking any traffic laws. So, being a young, full-of-himself attorney, I decided to teach him a lesson. I stared at his license plate which he knew meant that I was going to report him for something, so he charged me with bribery. For looking at his license plate! Police departments consider that to be a judgment call.

They threw me in jail with six degenerates who took turns urinating on me. I certainly learned my lesson! The cops let me use a phone and I called my boss and woke him up. My boss was a very wealthy man and was one of the most respected lawyers in town. You don't call a man like that to bail you out of jail. Not in the middle of the night and especially not when you're the low man on the totem pole at work. I'm not sure why I didn't call anybody else but I felt like I had no other choice. He came and bailed me out. The next day, I apologized to him in the office and he said nobody who worked for him ever had an experience like that. He also said he never had to bail anyone out. "That must be very embarrassing for you," he said. I told him he had no idea.

My ADHD made it difficult for me to concentrate and to get through college and law school. I had to do double and sometimes triple the work. I also had two jobs during law school. I flunked the bar exam because of my ADHD and also because the exam was a week or two after I finished law school. I would have been better served by waiting a few months until the next bar exam.

My brother was already a lawyer and we worked together at an automobile insurance company. I was a claims adjuster for the firm while he was one of its two attorneys. He got me the job. He never arrived before noon which always caused his partner to take his court call at the last minute. To his credit, my brother always stayed until midnight. I ended up working as an associate lawyer for him and his partner. I was always stuck with the court calls without any information because he didn't show up until noon. I made a fool out of myself every morning and was bawled out in front of the judges. I worked for them for about five years. At that point, I was in demand because of my claims adjuster experience and one of the most prestigious defense counsel firms hired me. They owned an insurance company and they knew my experience would be a great asset to them, which it was.

I really cut my legal teeth working for a top Personal Injury firm. They were "chasers," ambulance chasers. The two partners were sleeping with all of the secretaries every day of the week. Two weeks after being hired there, one of the partners asked me to come into his office. One of the secretaries was with him and he offered me the use of her body. I was quite shocked by the offer and I politely declined. Later, the same guy asked my wife to go to bed with him, because he knew we were having difficulty having children. I think my bosses looked upon themselves as a full-service law firm of sorts. Ultimately, these two guys were disbarred for paying off judges. I remember seeing one of the partners at a Tastee Freeze. As I approached, he yelled out, "Whatever you do, just realize that the girl in my car is my broad and not my wife." It turned out it was his wife. I think the guy felt like he had to laugh at his own jokes, because nobody else did.

In personal injury cases, you don't get to talk to anybody but your own client and your own witnesses, and it's sometimes three years before the jury trial comes up. There's little communication with clients and I didn't like that. I was a people person. I eventually moved into divorce law where I could talk to people about their problems. I was able to help them but I continued to do some personal injury cases to help keep my staff busy and to pay some bills.

Most divorce attorneys won't talk to a client on the phone. I do the opposite. I talk to them and they think they have a friend and so they come in to see me. But if I ask them what the date of their marriage is, they'll answer with non sequiturs like "it was raining outside and he wasn't supposed to see me on the day of the marriage. He came over anyway with a limo. His umbrella broke as he was getting out of the car and it ripped his tuxedo." I don't want to hear all that because I have another 15 questions to ask them and I don't have all day to spend on the phone. I ask them to give me one word answers, mostly yes or no. I explain why and they abide by that and they find that I'm very quick to the point and they like that I am. If they don't, it tells me they shouldn't be my client.

Divorce law takes a big toll on attorneys. Marriages fail all the time. I've been married twice. I married my first wife at the age of 27 and we divorced two years later. All my friends were getting married at the time and I felt the pressure was on me. I've thought about it a lot and I realized that my first marriage failed, because I was too controlling. Also, only big things bothered me. What bothered my first wife were things like a leaky faucet. The sex was never good and she wanted kids. I wasn't making much money yet so I used a condom all the time. She turned me on at first but my brain turned me off. I had other priorities. Success was more important to me than love and happiness. Plus, there was the inner fight going on within me between my brain and reality. I was single for three years.

I met my second wife on a coffee date. Actually, she was my fourth coffee date of the night. I guess that's a good way to meet people, particularly if you have little or no intent on getting to know them. But I got lucky when I met Donna. I've always loved her, but I used my work to limit my emotional contact with her as much as I could. I guess you could say I outlived my parents, but I didn't survive them. I suspect that other people feel the same way about their parents.

Looking back on our marriage, I'd change some things if I could. I used to get up at 3:30 in the morning, work out at the gym and be in my office by 6:30. I worked every Saturday and half of Sunday. If I could do things over, I'd be more relaxed, less intense less business like, and come home from work earlier. I'd take more vacations and be more relaxed with people. I have a lot of guilt about not being the husband and father I could have been. I suppose most men feel that way, the difference being the degree to which they rate their behavior. I thought I was being charitable by giving myself a D-minus because I wasn't entirely sure I deserved a passing grade. I guess it's a lot easier to recognize the value of forgiveness when you're the one who's asking for it.

Chapter 29

———————

SAVING MY MARRIAGE

Donna and I decided to put off the divorce for six months. I was surprised at her generosity in granting me this request. Perhaps it was because she realized the nature and character of the person who had tried to ruin our lives. After all, it was a form of entrapment that got me involved in Afshan's tangled web of lies. Maybe my wife realized that testosterone is not a character flaw. To a lot of men, it's their Achilles Heel. I had done nothing wrong. Then again, maybe my wife was just tired of the drama and the toll that this incredible journey had taken on her and the kids. Surely, there must have been something good about our marriage, something that gave her pause and allowed her to reconsider what may have been a rash, though understandable reaction on her part.

It was like getting to know each other all over again. I made no assumptions about what she might be thinking. Perhaps all the years that I was totally immersed in my work had left me with a rather superficial knowledge of who Donna really was, and how she had changed over the years. I believe that happens in a lot in marriages. People reach a point where they stop taking in new information and stop noticing changes in their spouse's behavior. They listen to what she said but they don't hear. If this sounds familiar to you, you're probably not alone. But if you don't start changing your ways, chances are you'll end up being very alone, whether your marriage survives or not.

Look, life's tough and then it gets incredibly difficult. The worst thing anyone can do to or for themselves is to put their life on automatic pilot. You know, just sort of going through the motions, rather than putting in the effort that a loving and committed relationship needs in order to thrive. Putting your car on cruise control on a road trip is fine, but putting your family life on automatic pilot will not only kill your marriage, it'll deaden your spirit. If you think otherwise, you're in denial. Just keep in mind that it's so easy to see what ails someone else's marriage and it's so freaking difficult to see what's wrong with your own.

After a few weeks, laughter returned to the Walters household. Our family dinners were unpredictable. When my children came over they were more engaged in the conversations than they used to be. There had been a small but detectable seismic shift in our family dynamics. My kids displayed a level of confidence in themselves that either hadn't been there before, or I had simply been too engrossed in my job to even notice. Whatever power I had lost in my role as father had apparently been scooped up by them and my wife. Actually, I really like the ring of that statement. No power had been lost, just reconfigured among all five family members. It's ironic that one of the most important lessons my kids learned from me was quite unintentional. It was situations like these that helped renew my self-esteem and reestablish my focus on the only thing that mattered to me - my family, and the love we felt towards each other.

Donna was the key to everything now. I had to earn my way back into her heart, just as I did when we fell in love. It wasn't enough just to talk the talk anymore, I had to walk the walk. It sounds easy enough to do in theory, but in reality, you can't go from A to Z in one fell swoop. Generally speaking, you get to Point Z one letter at a time.

It's funny how the great memories are never far from your consciousness. When my wife and I laid all our fears, disappointments, recriminations and feelings of betrayal aside, it was as if we were getting to know each other for the first time. We learned things about each other that we didn't know before. And, there certainly was a lot we didn't know about each other! OK, I admit she didn't learn as many new things about me as I did about her, but she had quite a few epiphanies herself. The things that were good about our marriage were the things we fell back on. We began to enjoy our give-and-take banter again, because I checked my sarcasm, or most of it, at the door. We were basically smoothing out all of our rough edges in an organic way. I guess what I mean by that is it was natural again; we weren't forcing issues and we weren't laying blame. Again, that was most generous on my wife's part because the blame was all mine. If I hadn't accepted that blame, and by that I mean ALL OF IT, our attempt at reconciliation would have been dead on arrival.

As a family, the kids, Donna and I went to Coney Island, a place that had long since lost its popularity with the general public. It was comparable to what Times Square looked like in the late 1970s and early 1980s. It was a seedy and desperate place, tolerable only because it was familiar and you were with your family or friends. But it was there that I had an epiphany. It was as if Coney Island was a microcosm of my situation. Like the amusement park, I hadn't worked on our problems because I didn't acknowledge their existence in the first place. Looking around at this once proud and universally popular amusement park made me realize that restoring it to its former luster was a far more daunting challenge that what our family was facing. Look, when you're grasping for straws, you often grab onto first thing you can. As pathetic as my analogy about Coney Island may sound, to me it was like giving sustenance to a very hungry man. When you're hungry, you take whatever food you can find. After all, beggars can't be choosers.

There's a limit to the value one should attach to the status quo, a term which is either positive or negative, depending on the situation. Accepting change is accepting the notion that nothing about day-to-day life is written in stone. Relationships can change when only one person changes. The one who changes sees what's happening; the one who doesn't change tends not to be aware of it. It's the proverbial fork in the road that puts two people on different paths. The good news for me was that I was finally realizing the truth about myself and our relationship. We could, if you believed in mini-miracles, make our bonds even stronger than before. At this point in my life, I couldn't afford not to believe that.

Life can indeed be incredibly difficult, and that's even without somebody trying to destroy you. I hadn't fully understood the depth of Afshan's malevolence until she finally realized that her husband had gotten the better of her in their divorce proceedings. If she couldn't hurt him or his girlfriend, she decided to inflict the maximum amount of damage on her favorite punching bag: little old me.

Chapter 30

BOMBSHELL DEJA VU

Afshan had sought my counsel a second time regarding the behavior of her ex-husband's girlfriend. A woman who is interested in a man with children wants to establish her own status in their household. She's trying to cement their relationship, and the best way to do that is through his children. The lawyer I recommended to Afshan filed a petition with the courts, asking that the girlfriend be admonished for having his children call her 'mommy.' Few ex-wives wouldn't be infuriated at such behavior, but most of them accept the situation and try to deal with it as best they can. Afshan wasn't one of them.

While that litigation was pending, Belin didn't get up one morning. He wasn't being lazy, he was being dead. An autopsy proved he had been poisoned, most likely the night before he died. The police tracked Belin's every movement over the previous month and tried to learn if he had any enemies. They grilled his girlfriend to find out her personal history and behavior before and after she became involved with Belin. She wasn't a prime suspect, but she was a suspect nevertheless.

Afshan was the prime suspect in this case. An investigation revealed that Belin met with her at her house where she poisoned his food. The police took samples from all unwashed plates in her apartment and searched the kitchen and bathroom for arsenic or some other potentially deadly substance. She was suspect number one, two and three and the police grilled her for hours, hoping to produce some testimony that might shed light on her and her motives. Little Miss Cleavage came equipped to the proceedings with Plans B, C, D, E, F and G. Guess whose name was invoked in Plan B?

Afshan claimed she had an accomplice in the murder of her husband, She maintained she only did what she did because I told her I'd kill her if she didn't kill him. She said I was crazy in love with her, that I couldn't stop thinking about her, and that I said no no-account of an ex-husband was going to prevent me from having all of her. "Damn the law," I supposedly said to her. "You belong to me now and you're going to kill your ex-husband." Have you ever heard such rubbish in your life? Apparently, the police had not.

I was talking to my wife when my secretary came into my office to deliver an urgent message. We had a method of non-verbal communication that she would employ if I was occupied with other business and she needed to get my attention quickly. What she usually did to convey this was to grab her neck with one of her hands. That told me my attention was needed elsewhere and that it was needed soon. On this particular morning, my secretary came into my office, put both hands around her neck, lied down on the floor and pretended to expire. I told Donna I loved her and got off the phone. My secretary's performance was so comical that I began to laugh, until I remembered that she was essentially a humorless person. At that moment, I figured I was in trouble.

She walked Detectives Schooner and Barnett into my office. We introduced ourselves and shook hands. "We'll get right down to the point, Mr. Walters," said Barnett. "The husband of one of your clients was murdered day before yesterday and we need you to account for your whereabouts that night." Never underestimate what the power of surprise can do. Cops know it all too well. From the moment they first lay their eyes on a possible suspect, they're trying to read that person. They know how to create a situation to elicit the greatest possible shock from a person of interest. Your first reaction is like gold to them and they use it to formulate their plan of attack. I knew this and my demeanor gave them nothing. I was scared to death but I didn't look the part.

"What's the name of my client?" I asked. As I'm saying this to them, the words, "Not Afshan, not Afshan, not Afshan" reverberated in my head. "Afshan Hassan," was the answer. I'm thinking to myself that on one level this is pretty funny. If this ever happens to you, try to remember that you're either experiencing the calm before the storm or you're actually in the eye of the hurricane itself.

"Mr. Walters," said Detective Schooner, "how would you characterize the relationship between your client and her husband." Before he even finished his sentence, I knew Afshan was their prime suspect. I hate to say it but I wasn't at all surprised. I knew her to be a woman who would stop at nothing to get her way. Since she so rarely got her way, she put no boundaries on her behavior. At that moment, I knew very well that I should be prepared for anything. "Gentlemen, I'd like to answer all your questions, but I only have 10 minutes before my next appointment. If that's all you think you'll need, let's continue. If not, I'd like to do this at a time that's convenient for both of us." We spoke for a few minutes and they thanked me for my time. They left with the perfunctory, "If we need anything else, we'll get back to you." There was something about the way Barnett looked at me that I found troubling.

It was deja vu all over again when I saw the story on the Six O'Clock News. This time, however, it was Afshan's face on the television screen. She had been charged with first-degree murder, rather than something serious like trying to seduce her attorney. "What a fucking idiot she is," I thought to myself. I used to tell people she was my client from hell. Now I was beginning to think she ran the place.

Then it hit me. I remembered that Afshan was always in control of herself whenever I interacted with her. She might get dramatic at times, even overly so, but it always seemed like she was acting. She was playing a part she was comfortable with; the beautiful, vulnerable, unappreciated wife and mother who spends her life warding off the unwanted advances of men. She secretly longed for love, but got none. Catch my drift? She did whatever she needed to do to cast herself as the helpless victim, lest anyone recognize her for the black widow she really was.

Did she really think she could get away with murdering her husband on a night when he was at her place for dinner? Did temporary insanity cause a crime of passion? As far as I could tell, Afshan was devoid of passion. She tried to fake it but it always rang hollow. Why then, I kept asking myself, would she paint herself into a corner from which there really was no escape?

I got the answer to my question the following morning when Detectives Schooner and Barnett paid me another visit. "My Walters, you're being charged with conspiracy to commit murder. You have the right to remain silent," said Schooner as he put the handcuffs on my wrists behind my back. "Everything you say can be used against you. You have the right to an attorney. Should you be unable to afford one, one will be appointed for you by the court. Do you understand your rights?" Actually, my rights were the only thing I understood at that particular moment.

The two detectives kept talking to me but I was lost in my thoughts. First came the anger over being accused of and arrested for a crime for which I could not possibly have been involved in. People can accuse anybody of anything, but they need to have hard and fast evidence to back up their contention before the police will act on the information. Afshan had nothing of the kind to involve me in any way, shape or form to the murder of her husband. From the time of our last meeting, there was nothing at all between us to back up her claim. She had called me on two or three occasions "just to say hello." Those were her words. We spoke no more than three minutes on any of those calls. That was the sum total of our contact.

I don't remember getting into and out of the police car. If they said anything at all to me from the time they put the cuffs on until the time we got to the police station, I have no recollection of it. They must have thought I was too scared to speak. They must have been fucking morons. I'd had enough of this woman. I decided to control the situation as best I could.

"Would you detectives please tell me what I'm being charged with?" I said calmly.

"We'll ask the questions here, Mr. Walters, not you," said a smirking Schooner.

"Gentlemen, there is one question on the table here, and it is the one I just asked you," I said. "If you choose not to answer it, I'd like to call my attorney."

"Hey Mike, check out the big brain on Phil. We may need to call for reinforcements," said Barnett.

"Good idea, Mensa man," I said, "and get your SWAT team while you're at it. And then get me a fucking phone."

There was silence and an absence of smirks for several seconds. For those few moments at least, I think they thought I was crazy. And if there's one thing I know about members of law enforcement, it's that they're more afraid of crazy people than they are of anyone else. You never know what a crazy person is going to do or what that person is capable of doing. It's outside most people's frame of reference. So, even though I was under arrest, they were a little less sarcastic now than they usually were. "Book the son of a bitch," is what they're probably thinking. It's like I always say, if you dish it out, you better be prepared to take it.

Four hours later, I was free on bail. I have never felt as strong or as resolute as I felt when Donna bailed me out of jail. As we walked arm and arm to our car, I could tell she held me differently than she did before. I felt affection, compassion and support in her touch and her look. There had been a major change in our interaction. Whatever Donna thought of me, she knew I could not kill somebody, nor could I plot with somebody to do it. The fact that these charges came from the woman who already tried to ruin me made everything clear to Donna.

My family pooled their resources to bail me out. I may have forgotten to mention that the bond was $2 million, meaning I had to post 10% of the amount, or $200,000. All they had on me was the word of their main suspect, and that was good enough for them to treat me like a serial killer. In so doing, they made this case big news, and that made me big news. Nobody wanted anything to do with me. Appearances really are everything. And once information is out there about you, it doesn't matter if the information is a lie and is recanted by the liar. The damage has already been done.

Here's a good example of what I mean. I was at a Judge's reception one night when I saw Ed Clark, the most influential member of New York City's City Council. He was in line getting a drink when I tapped him on the shoulder and said, "I'd like to introduce myself, Mr. Clark. I'm Phil Walters." I'll never forget the look on his face when he saw me. "Everybody knows who Phil Walters is!" said Clark. "How do you know?" I asked him. "Fuck! I read the newspaper every day and I can't avoid seeing your goddamn picture," he said. Back then, everybody in town would open the newspaper and see my picture on the third page. They used the picture from my advertisement in the phone book. This was worse than a nightmare because you get to wake up from nightmares. Then again, I had so much name identification as a result of this case, I could have run for office. "Vote for Walters," my slogan would say, "He's a victim just like you."

A preliminary hearing was held and the court determined they had enough evidence to sustain a charge of murder. So now I had to retain a criminal lawyer. I had gotten to the point where I needed to start printing money to get through this quagmire. But lacking the wherewithal to counterfeit hundred dollar bills, I had to count on the kindness of family members, none of whom were happy at the prospect. Unfortunately it costs just as much to defend yourself if you're innocent as it does if you're guilty.

Chapter 31

POSTING BAIL

I had given a lot of thought in trying to understand what kind of a person Afshan was and what made her tick. It may have been a sort of fool's errand, because the only things I had to go on were her behaviors towards me, her husband, and everybody else in her life. You can learn a lot that way but you can only learn so much. The last thing she was about to reveal to me or anybody else were her feelings. She probably learned the wisdom of that strategy in Iran where women knew better than to make their feelings known, lest they be seen as contrary and impertinent. Such bad behavior could result in repeated and increasingly bad beatings at the hands of her husband.

I came to the conclusion that Afshan was incapable of experiencing happiness. What passed for happy in her universe was making other people more unhappy than she was. If she didn't get what she wanted, she would make sure that you got what you didn't want. If she thought you were happy with your lot in life, it infuriated her to the point where she would do or say anything to blow it up. Until now, her weapon of choice was lying. But when her ex-husband came out of their marriage unscathed and better off than he was before, lying was no longer a suitable reaction.

I got so much publicity that I could have filled two small albums with all the press clippings. Seeing my picture in the newspaper was like looking into a mirror. The coverage could be classified into three major categories: bad, terrible, and catastrophic. It got to the point where I'd read something that belonged in the bad category and tell people it was good news. There's a saying that everything in life is relative. At that point in my life, everything was relatively bad.

My arraignment had the atmosphere of a media circus. This was a case straight out of a dime novel. Sex, power and death all rolled into one juicy little legal package. Ordinary murders generally attract little attention, especially if the principals are poor or immigrants. But the way the prosecutors were spinning this story was designed to have me convicted in the court of public opinion long before the trial began.

My lawyer told me not to respond to any questions from reporters, which is something I already knew. Ask me if the sun is shining and I'd say, "No comment." Ask me if I feel I'm being falsely accused and I'd say, "No comment." One female reporter asked me if I liked seeing my victims suffer. "No comment," was my reply. Of course, when you avoid answering a reporter's questions, many people think it's because you have something to hide. Forget that silly old notion that a defendant is presumed innocent until proven guilty. If the reporter tries to pay you back for your unwillingness to cooperate by putting in their own little spin in the articles, a presumption of guilt is quite common, especially among readers who prefer easy answers over complicated riddles.

Getting out of the courthouse gave new meaning to the term 'running the gauntlet.' The only parts of my body that seemed to be working were my legs and my eyes. I was zigging and zagging so much that I felt like I was running with a football. I was trying to avoid contact with anybody other than my wife and my attorney. The main thing was to keep moving forward. I couldn't control much about the situation I was in, but leaving the building as quickly as possible had to be one of the things that I could. I know how this sounds - I'm giving myself a lot of credit for being able to leave a building! Frankly, I don't blame you for laughing. Then again, I had just been indicted for murder. Trust me - if you ever find yourself in a situation even remotely similar to mine, locking yourself in your bedroom closet might seem to be a necessary and comforting move.

The effect on my firm's business was devastating. Most of our clients, at least the ones who knew me personally, were very understanding. However, let's just say that new clients weren't exactly flocking to us in droves. It was as if the hose had been turned off and all we had to sustain ourselves with was the water still in the hose. My staff knew a shake-up of personnel was coming soon and two of my employees, including one of my attorneys, quickly found jobs with other firms. A week after my arraignment, I called another staff meeting but this time I made

it the last order of business on a Friday, rather than the first order of business on a Monday, as I did before.

Five of my employees had been with me for 10 years. I had
always been straight with them, paid them a salary which was
higher than the industry average, and was there for them in
good times and bad. Though my other five employees had less
tenure, all but one of them were solid workers. That made the
problem of having to let four employees go a little easier, but not
by much. Two women on my staff had tears in their eyes even
before I began to speak.

Hoping to soften the mood in the room, I began by saying,
"Today's sermon is, 'How to Commit a Murder Without Even
Trying,'" That may have been the best line of my life because
within seconds everybody was laughing. The mood in the room
immediately changed. I think everybody knew that I could not
possibly have done what my client said I did. I wanted to convey
to all of them that I was alright, and that I had the inner strength
to deal with a situation I should have never had to deal with.

Even though I had been indicted for murder, I felt bad that
this would affect the lives of people on my staff. Laying off employees is an unpleasant job for many bosses. Rather than call
people into my office one person at a time, I told everyone I
would call them over the weekend to level with them about the
situation the firm was facing. I think they all appreciated how
sensitive I tried to be in this trying time. I say that because nobody left the office in tears, and also because every one of my
staff members either shook my hand or hugged me. When one
of the newer employees who I was about to lay off hugged me,

she said, "He touched my butt! I'm calling the DDC!" I laughed so hard that she asked me if I was alright.

Donna called me to ask when I planned on coming home. I told her I'd be there around six and she said she'd have dinner waiting for me. I told her it was one of the sweetest things she'd ever said to me and she was amused. I sat in my desk chair and looked around the office as if it were the last time I would see it.

When I got home, I received the surprise of my life. And this time, it was a good surprise. When I opened the front door, my friends and family descended on me with a show of love, affection and support that I had never experienced in my life. At that moment, things began to crystalize in my mind. By that I mean that everyone who knew me well, knew how preposterous the claim was that I had committed murder. Many of them were no doubt thinking that I was capable of cheating on my wife and that's why so many of them turned against me when the DDC put me on trial. But murder? It was as if Afshan had done me a favor of sorts, one which could be of long term value to me provided I didn't get convicted of murder. I could redefine my relationships with the people closest to me. They were sympathetic to me because they knew me.

I gave my wife such a passionate kiss that everybody applauded. After the kiss, my wife applauded and that brought the house down. Every day, Donna showed me in both little and big ways that she still had genuine feelings toward me. I had never been clearer on what was important to me than I was at that moment. This was my personal version of *It's A Wonderful Life* and I really felt that I was the richest man in town.

After everyone left, I began to cry. Donna didn't have to ask why. She came and sat next to me, kissed me on the cheek and rested her head on my shoulder. It was a perfect moment, though I'm not entirely certain which one of us fell asleep first. We slept for almost an hour. I woke up feeling liberated. Then I brushed my teeth and went to bed.

Chapter 32

REPRESENTING MYSELF

I t's been said that too much of a good thing can sometimes be bad. I think that's why they invented Mondays. Nevertheless, I actually slept an hour longer than I usually do and decided to bypass my gym workout to have breakfast with my wife. I felt a little like the hamster who manages to get himself off of the wheel every now and then. Of course, not understanding the wisdom and symbolism of that action, hamsters get right back on the path that goes nowhere. All I wanted to do with my wheel was to blow it to hell.

I told my secretary to screen all my calls because I didn't want to talk to the press. Apart from 22 phone calls and two personal visits, the members of the fifth estate managed to show real restraint. I called the attorney who represented me at my arraignment and told him I had decided to represent myself.

"Greg, only a fool has himself for a client," he said. "I never thought of you as a fool, before. If this isn't a joke, please tell me what the hell happened to you." I was pleased by his response.

"Well, Jim," I said, "When they drop the charges against me, and that will happen sooner than later, I want them to see that I didn't need anybody's help and was brave enough to risk - well, my life - to prove it." Jim said the perfunctory, "Well, I hope you know what you're doing, Greg." After a brief pause, he said, "Something tells me you do. Best of luck."

On the drive into work, I had remembered something my wife Donna said to me during my trials and tribulations with the DDC. "Greg," she said, "I've always wondered why you haven't protected yourself better from the kind of thing that's happening to you now." I asked her what she meant and she said, "Well, if I were an attorney, and I had a few clients like you-know-who, I'd record every one of my phone conversations with them and keep a meticulous log of the time and duration of each contact." I thanked her for the idea and I implemented it the very next day. And then I forgot all about it.

On my way into work I had an epiphany. Afshan's version of the facts was at odds with the content of the phone calls that I received from her. I never once called her, though she insisted I called often. Perhaps, in her frenzy to kill her husband, she didn't wait long enough to make certain that she had covered all of her bases with respect to my supposed role in her plan. It was unlike her to be that sloppy but I think her thirst for her husband's blood had, by this time, taken over her mind. Lucky for me.

I looked at my log of calls from her and listened to all of them. Afshan had grossly overplayed her hand by implicating me in her husband's murder. She had nothing to substantiate her charges against me, apart from her word and a log of a few, brief phone calls she made to me. That shouldn't have been enough to get me arrested so she must have come up with some real tasty embellishments to get law enforcement to take her claim seriously without even checking the facts. Who knows, maybe the cops and district attorney were more focused on her cleavage than they were on the legal process.

The tape recordings of her calls disproved every one of her accusations against me. Of course, and you probably know this, you cannot record someone without their permission. That meant these tapes would not be admissible in court, but that was fine in this case. That's because the prosecutor would not be able to proceed with the case against me knowing that my accuser had made it all up. If anything, Afshan's lies about me made the case against her almost airtight. She'd be lucky to get convicted on a charge of second-degree murder, because it was clear to everyone now that her crime had been premeditated.

After I got off the phone with my attorney, I leaned back in my chair, put my feet up on the desk, and enjoyed the best cup of coffee of my life. It was a beautiful, sunny day and a wave of optimism washed over me. I was no longer deep inside a tunnel, looking for that proverbial light. Something inside of me had changed and I was thankful for it. And then I did something I never do; I called my wife and told her I was taking the day off. "Where are we going?" she asked. "I haven't had time to even think about that," I replied. "But, wherever we're going, we're going together."

ABOUT THE AUTHOR

Army veteran Barry L. Gordon has been practicing law in Chicago, Illinois for 48 years. He was duly admitted and qualified to practice in front of the United States Supreme Court in 1979, and to the Northern U.S. District Court in 1982. He has specialized in matrimonial law for most of his career and provides legal services to more than 400 divorce clients each year. For the past 15 years, he has produced and hosted a local television program in Chicago, entitled *You And The Law*. Gordon is married and has two adult children. This is his first novel.

Made in the USA
San Bernardino, CA
27 July 2016